Orion:
Symbiont of Passion

By
Herbert Grosshans

Published by
Melange Books, LLC
White Bear Lake, MN 55110
www.melange-books.com

ISBN 978-1-61235-015-8
Orion: Symbiont of Passion
By Herbert Grosshans
Copyright © 2009, 2011

Credits

Editor: Nancy Schumacher
Copy Editor: Taylor Evans
Format Editor: Mae Powers
Cover Artist: A. Bratt

Orion:
Symbiont of Passion
By Herbert Grosshans

Agent Hektor Orion's mission takes him to Bakker's Planet where he has to find the people responsible for making one hundred sacrificial robot-virgins behave all too life-like. Orion may be more than human, but even his extraordinary abilities cannot save him from the influence of the Symbiont of Passion.

Visit Herbert's website:

http://hegro.shawwebspace.ca
http://hegro.blogspot.com/

Works also by and including Herbert Grosshans:

Stardogs 1 & 2
The Xandra Triology
Cliffs of Time
Orion the Hunt
Beyond the Stars Digest
Men of Eros

Orion: Symbiont of Passion
By Herbert Grosshans

Prologue

Tall and thin, Earl Preston looked frail behind his wooden desk, but Orion knew this to be an illusion. Only a strong, ruthless man could have risen to the position of Director of Planetary Control on this planet. Orando was the fifth planet in the *Orelli System*, highly industrialized and densely populated, mainly because of its location around the giant Primary. The seasons were moderate and the weather stable. An ideal planet, unlike the fourth and sixth. One of them hot and dry, the other one cold and harsh, with the large cities under huge protective domes.

"As you are aware, Agent Orion, Orando is best known for its electronic devices and robotic machines, which are manufactured by the majority of our larger companies. You probably don't know that the finest robots are built on Bakker's Planet, the sixth planet in our system. Since Bakker's Planet does not have much of a spaceport, all shipments out of the system go through Orando. Actually, most deals are made through Orando."

Preston leaned back in his oversized chair and took a long drag from a thin cigarette. He breathed out slowly through his nostrils and looked at the big man sitting across from him.

"Apex, our neighbor closer to the sun, was settled largely by groups of religious people. Once a year, after the winter season, they have a big celebration where they sacrifice young virgins to their god." Preston smiled thinly. "I know that practice is nothing new, but these people are civilized. For obvious reasons they can't use human girls, so they use dolls made from plastic, but this year they decided to make it more realistic and had young virgins made to order. One thousand of them. They were built according to specs on Bakker's Planet and delivered through us."

Orion didn't comment, wondering where this was heading.

"Somebody with a twisted sense of humor made these robots all too life-like," Preston continued. "There exists a small creature on Bakker's Planet which, at certain times, lives in symbioses with other

4

creatures. Our knowledge about it is limited; all we know is that this little animal possesses a strong sex-drive, which it transmits to its symbiotic partner. Some genius bio-technician implanted these creatures into the control circuits of the one thousand robot-virgins.

"Apparently, these tiny creatures are telepathic, and any male coming within range gets as horny as hell. You can imagine what happened on the great Day of Celebration. One thousand sex-driven virgins with the capacity to do so practically raped most of the males present, and there were thousands of them. It was probably the largest orgy a religious gathering ever witnessed."

Orion smiled, but his gray eyes remained cool. "I really don't understand why a government agent of the Colonial Worlds of Sol-Terra had to be called in for that. It seems like a small local problem to me."

"It would have been, but understandably the people of Apex, especially the women, were furious. Since they dealt with Orando, they directed their anger at us. They kidnapped one of our passenger cruisers and gave us an ultimatum: Find out who is responsible for the cruel joke or all of the people on board the cruiser will be killed. One of the passengers happens to be our president's daughter. You see the problem? If anything happens to her it will mean war." Preston stared at Orion. "They also demanded that an outside party be brought in to handle the investigation."

Orion nodded thoughtfully. "I see," he said. He stood up and walked over to the large window overlooking the city. In the distance, he could see the long, thin needle-shaped spaceships breaking through the clouds.

He was a big man. Tall, lean-hipped, with wide shoulders. Under his tight-fitting black clothes, his muscles rippled as he moved gracefully across the thick carpet. The Director's gaze rested for a brief moment on the large energy pistol strapped to the big man's hip.

"I have made arrangements for you to go to Bakker's Planet. You'll be met by a local agent. Officially, you are a wealthy merchant who wants to buy a certain kind of robot. My secretary will supply you with your ID and a specially prepared chip." He joined Orion by the window, looked at the city below. "We haven't had a war for a hundred years, Agent Orion. This problem needs to be resolved peacefully." He held out his hand. "Good Luck."

5

Chapter One

Orion arrived at the small spaceport near North-City in the late afternoon. An air-cushioned vehicle took him to his hotel in the domed city. Even though it was late spring on Bakker's Planet, it didn't make any difference, because the climate inside the domes was always the same.

He stepped off the elevator and walked down the carpeted corridor toward his suite. Pressing his hand against the scanner in the doorframe, the door opened silently to reveal a large, richly furnished suite, one befitting a wealthy merchant.

Walking through the door leading into the bedroom, he stopped abruptly when he sensed the presence of someone in the room. His hand reached for the small weapon concealed inside his coat, but he didn't draw it when he saw the woman.

She lay on top of the big bed.

Completely nude.

"Who are you?" he asked, studying her naked body.

She smiled and slid off the bed. When she walked toward him, her hips swayed seductively. He noticed her large breasts. Firm and solid, they hardly moved on her ribcage. Her long, copper-colored hair hung loosely around her creamy shoulders.

Staring at the small fuzzy triangle between her long, slim legs, his eyes traveled back to her face, noted its perfect shape. Almost too perfect, too beautiful.

Her pink tongue ran over her red, full lips. Stepping close to him, she said with a sultry voice, "Compliments of the hotel. I am here for your pleasure."

He smelled her faint perfume, but something about her didn't seem right. "You are a robot," he said.

Smiling, she nodded and put her slim arms around his neck. "Yes and no. I am not cold steel and plastic. I'm different. My body was grown artificially to make it soft and warm for your ultimate pleasure. I have been programmed for anything you want me to do. I can make all your fantasies come true." Her lips touched his. They felt warm and soft.

Human.

He pushed her away, gently. As beautiful and desirable as she appeared, she was artificial, and he didn't really care to have intercourse with a robot.

She pulled a face. "You don't like me, sir?"

Orion admired this marvel of engineering. He had seen robots before, of course, but never one as lifelike as this one. "I don't want to interfere with your programming. You are extremely beautiful and I like you, but I have other things to do right now. Be a good girl and mix me a drink."

He watched her walk into the living room, admired the movement of her round naked buttocks.

"Damn it!" he cursed under his breath. "Am I getting aroused by a machine?"

She looked back over her shoulders, her long lashes fluttering. On a sudden impulse, his mind reached out and he cursed loudly when he made contact, realizing why he had been able to sense her presence.

Her mind closed almost immediately. She turned and looked at him with large eyes. "You are a telepath," she said, her voice still soft and seductive, but with a different tone.

Three steps took him close to her and he spun her around roughly. "Who the hell are you and why are you masquerading as an artificial?"

"I am Azalee, your contact," she said, looking into his angry face. "This body, which you are admiring, is artificial, an android, but I am not. I am inside this head, behind these pretty blue eyes."

This time it was she who reached out and he felt the probing touch. Carefully and on guard, he blended his thoughts with hers and was astonished at the strong mind he found.

I can explain much better this way," she said, using only her thoughts.

He *saw* a small, shapeless being inside the brain cavity of the android.

I am only partially physical and I need a host body to survive. Half of me is what you would describe as an electric current. That gives me the ability to control this synthetic product. To me this android is like a real body. When it is damaged, I feel the pain. When it experiences pleasure, I feel it too.

Are there more like you? Orion asked.

Only a few. She looked at him, her lovely face serious. *I feel I can trust you. I am not a native of this part of the Galactic Wheel. We came in a space vessel from the other side of the Galaxy. We crashed on this planet. Not many of us survived. Our host bodies could not live in the atmosphere of this planet, so for a while we inhabited the bodies of local animals, until we found the humans.*

Our ethics forbid us to take over the body of an intelligent creature, so we decided to have our own host bodies built for us. The human form was the most logical and practical.

She smiled and came closer. "I enjoy physical contact as much as you do and I have all the necessary equipment." She kissed him hungrily and pulled him toward the bed.

He felt himself responding and let her undo his belt. Reaching into his pants, she laughed when she found him hard and curled her fingers around his manhood. Then she undressed him slowly and almost tenderly.

When he was naked, he took her into his strong arms and stretched her out on the bed.

"You did not tell me anything about yourself," she whispered, "but I can sense something strange about you. Something that pulls me toward you. I almost feel as if you and I have much in common. Your body is human, but your mind is more than that, much more."

She didn't know how close to the truth she had come, but Orion kept his inner thoughts to himself. There was no need at this time to reveal too much.

Sighing deeply, she opened her thighs wide and carefully guided him inside.

He felt the slippery softness closing around his erect penis and the gentle pressure of her hands on his hips. They moved silently for a long time. Their minds touched and flowed together, and even though she had a synthetic body, she was as alive and human as any woman who had ever coupled with him.

When she started to whimper, he grabbed her soft buttocks and crushed her to him, driving his hard pole into her with long, deep strokes.

Her body twisted and churned under him. She cried out, her fingernails raking his back. His discharge shot into her like an erupting geyser and she lifted her buttocks off the bed to meet his thrusts. She clamped her long legs around his torso and they stayed motionless until his penis stopped pumping. She quivered beneath him, experiencing her own orgasm, and he had to admit, she was a perfect love machine.

When the pleasure slowly subsided, she relaxed and sighed loudly.

That was beautiful, she said inside his mind, and then she kissed him on the tip of his nose.

As their bodies untangled, their minds also drew apart. They both understood the need for privacy.

He lay back and closed his eyes. "This was not really the kind of contact I expected," he said, turning his face toward her when she laughed.

"They briefed me about you and I wanted to see how tough you really are," she said, smiling, her fingers trailing across his deep chest.

"I guess you've discovered my weakness." He grinned and took her into his arms.

Chapter Two

The next day Azalee arranged for him to meet with a man named Cal Thalson, the Chief of Security of the largest robot manufacturing company, ELCOM.

Thalson turned out to be a big, beefy man with hard looking eyes. He didn't smile much. "You seem to be on the level, Mr. Orion. According to our information, you do indeed own part of the planet *Athena*. Even though it is just a small backwater planet in the *Minolka System*, you are a rich man. Now it is up to our sales department if we want to deal with you."

He paused and added, "Not many deal directly with us."

Orion smiled. "My needs are of a somewhat delicate nature and I would prefer to deal with the president of ELCOM himself."

Thalson lifted his hand, a disgusted look on his face. "Impossible, Mr. Orion. General Okten does not get involved in any business dealings, unless it is government business. I don't believe you realize that General Okten practically owns Bakker's Planet."

He leaned forward. "Let me put it in other words: General Okten *is* Bakker's Planet. He has no time for trivial things like this."

"If he is so busy then he probably doesn't even know what goes on in his company," Orion said.

Thalson looked at him sharply. "What do you mean by that?"

"Nothing. You see, I didn't send any of my employees to conduct this business. I came here myself and I don't want to deal with just anybody. Only with the top man."

"Mr. Abhalla handles the more important deals. He is General Okten's right hand." Thalson sighed heavily. "I'm afraid you'll have to be satisfied with him."

Orion shrugged. "Very well then. When can I see this Abhalla? My time is limited and I am anxious to get on with my business." He gave Thalson a thin smile. "Even though *Athena* is a backwater planet, I own a large chunk of it and I am also a busy man."

* * * *

They met with Mr. Abhalla within the hour. He was a small, dark-skinned man with a bright, flashing smile. He shook hands with Orion jovially and offered him a big cigar. Orion declined, watched Abhalla light his own and puff out great clouds of smoke.

Abhalla looked at Azalee and nodded approvingly. "I see you love perfection, Mr. Orion. This model here was not made in our laboratories, but by one of our competitors. Nevertheless, she is a beautiful thing to look at. She could easily pass for human and..." he winked knowingly, "I am sure she performs well. However, you will not regret coming to us. We can match anything our competitors build. I dare say, we produce a better product and at a lower price."

He rubbed his hands. "Now, Mr. Orion, without mincing too many words, what exactly can we do for you?"

Orion pulled a small computer chip out of his pocket and handed it to the black man. Abhalla pushed it into a slot in his desk and watched the hologram take form.

Even Orion winced when he saw the three-dimensional images on top of the desk.

Young, naked girls locked in deep embrace with half-naked men, their tunics carelessly pushed up past their waists. Hundreds of girls, lying on their backs, their white legs spread apart and the men throwing themselves between those inviting thighs. Between the writhing bodies, women, dressed in long robes, were trying to pull the men off the girls, unsuccessfully.

The black man's face showed no expression when he looked at Orion. "I don't understand the purpose of this, sir."

When Orion carefully tried to probe his mind, he received nothing but gibberish. Abhalla wore a thought scrambler. Not unusual for a man in his position. Orion smiled. "Those girls are robots, supposedly built by your company, Mr. Abhalla, but I guess you know that."

"Of course I recognize our product and I know all about this incident, Mr. Orion." Abhalla spoke coldly, suspicion in his voice. "They were of a superior design, but somebody tampered with the programming. Not our fault. How did you get a hold of this?" He indicated the computer chip.

"That is really of no importance." Orion spread his hands. "Enough money buys anything." He leaned forward. "I want one hundred female robots, programmed for one purpose only...sex. One hundred love machines. As beautiful as Azalee, my companion. They must be able to arouse a man and keep him under their spell. It can be done. These pictures prove it. I also want them to be tied to a control unit so they can be monitored and manipulated from one central point. Pictures and sound."

11

Orion leaned back, folding his hands. "Money is no object."

"I'm sure it isn't," Abhalla said dryly. "What you request is not impossible, but we cannot build a robot to hypnotize a human being. What happened on Apex is a mystery to us. Someone apparently used Mongos to control those oversexed virgins. I'm sure you know everything about that. Unfortunately, that is beyond our capabilities. Besides, it is also against the law."

"The law," Orion said. "Come, come now, Mr. Abhalla. Mr. Thalson told me General Okten pretty much owns Bakker's Planet. Doesn't that mean he also makes the law? I'm certain we can work out something."

"I'm afraid not, Mr. Orion."

* * * *

The small air-cushioned vehicle sped silently down the only road toward the next city dome. Outside, small snowflakes fell lightly from the overcast sky. A heating grid below the road surface melted the flakes as soon as they touched, keeping the road dry at all times.

Orion leaned back into the cushions and stared across the snow-covered land. Not far in the distance, he could see the peaks of a mountain ridge reaching into the sky. "It sure looks bleak out there," he said to Azalee, who gave him a warm smile.

"The temperature outside is minus 12 Celsius at the moment. The forecast for tonight calls for minus twenty-five. May I remind you this is springtime? Don't forget though, we are in the northern hemisphere, where there is no snow for only about sixty days. We even get beautiful flowers growing when the snow melts."

"I wonder why anyone would want to live here." Orion felt a momentary chill, even though the heating unit made the interior of the vehicle pleasantly warm.

"Minerals," Azalee told him. "Especially the abundance of Krill-crystals, which are the building blocks for the robot power units. It is quite pleasant inside the domes, where we have gardens for leisure and for growing vegetables and fruit."

"Where do your people live?" Orion asked suddenly.

Azalee shrugged. "Scattered all over the planet. We lead a lonely life."

Something deep inside Orion stirred; that thing that made Orion different from other humans. Memories of past, half-forgotten lives flashed through his mind.

Yes, he knew about loneliness.

In many ways, he was like Azalee. How long ago had it been since his kind had come to this galaxy? He didn't really know. Humans had been primitive then, planet bound. However, he remembered his first human ancestor. A big hunk of a man, a hunter in the primeval forest of Earth, a small planet in a star system near the edge of the Galaxy.

The primitive's mind had merged with the energy being from another galaxy, one of many fugitives from the evil Hunters, who had followed them and were hunting them still through the millennia.

Orion sighed as he remembered. He had inherited the *Ancient Memory* from his biological father. He was a carrier, in a sense he was still Lord Kas, the High Lord, but he was also Horga, the hunter, or Derbus, the roman soldier, or Mr. Francois Daborion, the French adventurer. The list was endless. When his family moved to *Freedom* in the Sirius System, they changed the name to Orion.

He felt Azalee watching him and he took her hand into his. "I know how you must feel," he said.

She leaned over to kiss him. "You find me attractive?" she whispered.

"Yes, I do."

"Is it this pretty body?"

"No, not just that body. When we touched minds, I saw the beauty inside you. The real you. Since we are speaking of your body, I am wondering about something. How is it possible that you can be an agent? Surely, the authorities know that you are a construct."

"They do, but the people I work for also know that I am more than just an android. They know what I really am, and that's why I am so valuable to them."

"How would they know about you?"

She chuckled. "I can never hide from a telepath, and there are plenty of them around these days. You knew immediately that I was not just a collection of plastic and wires."

Orion looked outside. The snow came down heavy now and the wind seemed to have picked up. He studied the dark clouds moving across the sky. "Looks like a storm coming. I hope this vehicle can stay on the road."

Azalee laughed. No true android could produce a sound like that. It was full of emotion and almost human. "It would take the blast of an atomic bomb to dislodge us," she said.

The vehicle slowed suddenly and came to a dead stop. Without the gravity control device, the force would have flung them against the front windshield.

A dark shape loomed in front of them, blocking the road.

Two shadows came toward their vehicle, stopped beside it. One of them rapped against the side window.

"Security," a hard-edged voice came over their com. "Open up!"

Both Security men had artificial mind shields built into their helmets, but Orion didn't have to read their thoughts to know their intentions. When he stepped out of the vehicle, they confronted him with their energy guns drawn.

The icy air almost took away his breath, and he felt the cold wind cutting through his light clothing.

"Identification!" barked one of the men and waved his weapon in front of Orion's face. Very carefully, Orion reached inside his pocket and pulled out his ID disc. The security man barely glanced at it and pushed Orion against the vehicle.

"This one's an Artificial," said the second man, turning his back toward Azalee. As far as he was concerned, she didn't exist.

"You shouldn't be out in a storm," the one in front of Orion said with a sneering grin. "If you should experience a mechanical malfunction, you could freeze to death."

The other one laughed, shoved his gun through the open door of the vehicle, and put a burst of energy into the control panel. "Seems you've got a problem," he said with a wide grin. "It's three hundred kilometers to the nearest city and nothing in between but snow."

When Orion felt Azalee's mind-touch, he moved. His foot shot out and kicked the weapon from the security man's hand. It became instantly obvious the man was trained in unarmed combat. He lashed out with his booted foot, aiming for Orion's unprotected head.

Even though Orion was big, he possessed reflexes faster than an ordinary man did. Avoiding the kick easily, he fell back and attacked again. The cold was getting to him and he wanted to get it over with fast. He received a hard blow to the chest, and then he rammed his knee into the security man's belly. When his opponent doubled over, he brought the edge of his hand down hard against the man's neck.

Turning, he saw the second man collapse. Azalee stood over him, his weapon in her hand. "He made a fatal mistake treating me like an ordinary robot," she said.

"What should we do with them?" Orion asked.

"Kill them. They would have killed you."

"No, we can't do that. Not anymore. That would be cold-blooded murder. We rendered them helpless, the threat is gone." He looked at the smoldering ruins of their vehicle's control panel. "Is there any way we can send a distress signal?"

Azalee nodded, brushing the snow from her face. "It's automatic. They already know about the damage."

"Then let's put these two inside and we'll take their cruiser."

Chapter Three

Inside the police cruiser, Orion rubbed his face and shook the snow out of his dark hair. "I'm frozen to my bones," he said, watching Azalee fiddle with the controls.

"We'll have to move fast, before they can track us down," she said. "I've disconnect the monitor, but now they know that something is wrong. They'll send out someone to investigate."

The cruiser was much larger and roomier than the one they had abandoned. A couple of narrow bunks in the rear and a fold-down table made it clear that it was designed for spending time away from the city domes.

Azalee punched the co-ordinates of the next city into the computer and the cruiser made a turn and began moving west, picking up speed quickly.

Orion sat down on one of the bunks. After giving the controls one last check, Azalee joined him on the bunk. "We have maybe one hour," she said." Then we'll have to ditch this thing."

"We'll still be in the middle of nowhere by then." He gave her a puzzled look when she began to peel off her clothing.

She laughed when she saw him stare. Then she dropped the last peace of her garments.

He admired the smooth rippling of muscles, when she walked naked to a locker and pulled out a couple of uniforms. She threw one package at him and he caught it, putting it beside him.

Seeing Azalee's lovely form caused a sudden pounding in his loins. He stood up and took her into his arms, ran his hands up and down her smooth back, down to her rounded buttocks.

"Like you said, we have one hour." He grinned, one of his hands cupping her breast, kneading it gently.

Azalee's body may have been synthetic and her brain an alien creature, but she was all woman. The alien intelligence that was Azalee was female. Millennia of living in a host body and being telepathic had made her species different from others.

Azalee's psyche had easily adjusted to the human form and she found a human male quite attractive. Because of the mind link with Orion, it was even easier for her. When they had intercourse, not only their bodies joined but also their minds.

She responded quickly to his touch. Her breathing became heavier and she urged him toward the bunk. She helped him out of his clothes and pushed him onto his back. Straddling him, she grabbed his already hard and throbbing penis and eagerly guided it into the coppery floss between her open thighs.

He watched her greedy fleshy lips swallow up his pole and his thoughts flowed toward hers.

She smiled.

You feel good inside me. Her thoughts caressed him. *I have never coupled with a man who was a telepath. This is a completely new experience for me and I'm beginning to like it.*

A soft moan escaped her lips when Orion pushed himself deep into her. His strong fingers clamped around her hips, controlling her movements as she wildly gyrated above him.

"Easy," he said hoarsely. "Let's not hurry too much." Then his hands moved up to fasten on her large bouncing breasts. He squeezed them gently and she let out another loud moan.

Her hips moved slowly now, the muscles of her vagina milking him softly. "I think I'm ready," she said breathlessly after a while and pushed down hard when she felt his spermatic fluid shooting into her.

She whimpered like a wounded animal and Orion called out in a loud hoarse voice when their minds merged in the final climax. Falling on top of him, she lay unmoving, her breasts like two soft balls on his hard chest.

Again, Orion felt amazement for the creature he held in his arms. She was as much a woman as any he had ever known. He kissed her gently and she wrapped her arms around him tightly. Her long hair fell across their faces as she pressed her warm lips against his.

"Is it possible that I'm falling in love with you?" she whispered.

He became aware of her confusion.

"We must not let that happen," she said.

Orion stroked her copper-colored hair. "Let's just enjoy this moment and worry about everything else later."

She giggled when he put her onto her back and moved between her legs. "Are you ready again?" Pulling her knees up, she opened her legs wide and sighed happily when he entered her.

Their minds touched again, and for a long time they were silent, only their bodies communicated. They were hardly aware of the storm raging outside. Their sighs and moans drowned out the barely audible sounds filtering through the insulated walls of the cruiser.

Azalee bucked and heaved under him, as he snapped his hips back and forth, driving his swollen member as deep as possible into her with each stroke. When he climaxed, they both cried out at the same instant.

Covered with sweat, he lay panting on top of her. "You're draining me of all my energy," he said, breathing hard.

"That's where this body is superior to yours." She smiled. "I could go on all day." Pushing him gently off her, she slipped from the bunk and rummaged around in a cabinet. "Ah, here we are," she said, handing him a small package. "Energy tablets," she explained. "Take them."

"How about you?" he asked, and then he swallowed the two tablets. "How do you nourish your…your real body?"

"The same way you do." She popped a couple of tablets into her mouth. "Come on, get up and put this uniform on your handsome frame. It is a survival suit with a built-in heating unit. You'll need it when we go outside."

* * * *

"You're sure we're walking in the right direction?" Orion put his face close to Azalee's. They did not dare to use the com built into their helmets in case someone else picked up their transmissions.

Yes, she said in mind-speech.

Orion smiled. It was more natural for him to use the conventional human way of communication. Azalee, however, seemed to prefer the transfer of thoughts more and more.

They put their backs against the howling wind and rested for a while.

We should reach the settlement in about three, maybe four hours. We'll be safe there.

If we make it. Orion felt pessimistic. He trusted Azalee, but he didn't like to depend on her. He needed to be the one in charge.

We'd better get going.

Orion brushed the snow from his protective visor and looked at the gauge on his wrist.

Minus forty degrees with the wind.

If it weren't for the survival suits, he'd be frozen by now dressed in his light indoor clothing. Only about half an hour had passed since they left the police cruiser, but it felt as though they'd been walking for hours.

The wind whipped the snow across the frozen ground, covering their tracks almost as soon as they were made. It was slow going but he knew they couldn't stop. So far, the snow wasn't too deep, but at the rate it came down it wouldn't be long until walking through it would be nearly impossible.

"I hope you are right, Azalee," he murmured to himself, "because as far as I am concerned we are hopelessly lost."

He was barely able to see more than a meter ahead in the driving snow.

Azalee stopped suddenly and grabbed his arm. *Something just past us overhead. They're looking for us.*

Orion's com alive at the same time Azalee transferred her thoughts.

"This is Search and Rescue. We know you are down there, Orion. Turn on your homing signal and we will pick you up."

Don't answer your com. It is a trap, Azalee warned. *As soon as they have a fix on us, they'll kill us.*

How did they track us down? Orion wondered.

They must have found the abandoned police cruiser sooner than I thought. I never figured they'd send out air sleds in this storm. They know there are only two places we can head for to find shelter: The next city or the mountains.

Why do they need my signal to find us if they know we are here?

They don't really know where exactly we are. You just happened to pick up their transmission.

The com crackled again. "Please, turn on your homing signal, Mr. Orion. We just want to talk to you."

Turn off all of your electronic equipment, including your heating unit, Azalee suggested. *They might be able to find us that way.*

Orion had barely followed her suggestion, when a bright flash nearly blinded him and the force of the explosion made him stagger.

Too late. I think they found us.

He grabbed Azalee's hand and they started running. Another explosion close by threw them to the ground. A stab of sharp pain shot through his left leg and then he felt a dull thud against his head.

Suddenly, the world around him began to slip away and he seemed to be floating in darkness. His mind reached out toward the sled, searched for the pilot's mind, found it. With a last, desperate effort, he smashed the artificial mindshield, entered the other mind, and sent a commanding impulse. Before he lost consciousness, he heard the pilot's silent scream as the air sled crashed to the ground.

* * * *

A dull, throbbing pain in his left thigh brought him back to consciousness. He tried to move, but found he couldn't. Something held him down.

Opening his eyes, he looked around to find himself in unfamiliar surroundings.

He lay on a narrow bed, his body covered by a thin sheet. Wide straps tied around his upper and lower torso secured him to the bed.

The small room was sparsely furnished. It looked and smelled like a hospital room.

Carefully reaching out with his mind, he sensed the presence of others outside. Somebody was heading for the door to his room. A young woman, dressed in a plain white cotton dress entered the room.

She smiled when she saw him awake. "Good morning, Mr. Orion," she said brightly, stepping closer. Her black hair, tied into a ponytail, accented her wide cheekbones.

He noticed her pretty face and black sparkling eyes.

Her breasts swung freely inside the loose dress when she bent over him to unfasten the straps and he stared at the deep cleavage.

"Nice," he murmured. When he noticed the pink color creeping up her neck and cheeks, he grinned.

"I can see you are recovering," she said, smiling. "You were in bad shape when you were brought to us, with one broken leg, a deep gash in your thigh, and a concussion."

She examined the cast on his left leg. "I think we can remove that today. You are lucky we have a fully equipped hospital facility here or else you may have lost that leg. We had to use a lot of *plastaskin* to cover the wound in the thigh, but you'll be as good as new."

He realized that he was nude under the thin cover. Very casually, she pushed aside his penis when she removed the bandage from his thigh.

"It looks good," she said, and then she colored again when he grinned. "I'm talking about your leg, Mr. Orion. By the way, a bit more to the left and you would not be grinning so much now."

He watched her apply a new bandage with deft fingers and admired the outline of her trim figure against the bright sunlight falling through the window.

"How long have I been here?" he asked, serious now.

"Three days. We've kept you full of healing drugs and sedated to speed up your recovery."

"Where is Azalee?"

Her black eyes regarded him silently. "The lady who brought you? She left. A remarkable woman. How she managed to carry you through that terrible snowstorm is hard to explain. Without her, you surely would have perished."

"Where did she go? Did she leave a message?" Orion tried to sit up, but she pushed him back.

"Rest now. There is time for explanations later."

"What's your name?" he asked.

"Azur. Now you rest."

He wanted to touch her mind, but controlled the urge. It was against his ethics to snoop in other people's private thoughts, unless it was absolutely essential, so he just lay back and closed his eyes.

Later, she told him. There would be enough time later.

* * * *

He took a few steps, putting weight on his left leg and grinned at Azur who stood watching him. "As you promised, as good as new."

She smiled and uncovered a package she had brought with her. It contained a plastic cube. Something moved inside, a jelly-like transparent mass.

"This is a Mongo," she said. "You've heard of them? They live in symbiosis with the native population. For some reason, the males of the many tribes have a low sex-drive. It is practically non-existent. So, at the beginning of spring, the women go out and search for Mongos, which they put on their bodies, over their pubic area."

While she was talking, she took the jelly-like mass out of its container. Then, to Orion's surprise, she lifted the hem of her dress and pulled it over her head. Stark naked now, she laid the quivering mass on her flat stomach. "Like this," she said.

The Mongo flowed down her stomach to cover the black triangle between her legs, and then it slowly disappeared from view.

"A woman carrying a Mongo thus becomes irresistible to any male who comes close. The little creature is telepathic. It emits vibrations, which create a strong sexual urge in the male. The tribes have yearly fertility celebrations, where the women couple with different males to ensure they become pregnant." She smiled. "They also call the Mongo *Symbiont of Passion*."

Orion felt a strange sensation coming over him. "What about the Mongo? What does it get out of this?" he asked hoarsely, stepping closer to Azur.

Her eyes were bright when she looked at him. She had seemed pretty before, but now she was unbelievably beautiful. "It insures the Mongo's survival. After the man releases his sperm inside the woman's womb, the Mongo inserts nearly invisibly tendrils into the woman's sex-canal and sucks up some of the spermatic fluid." She laughed. "That's how little Mongos are made."

Orion took another step. He felt an urge in him that he couldn't control. Azur stood like a nude goddess, smiling radiantly. Her skin was smooth and coppery, her breasts firm and high, her legs long and slim. The black fuzzy triangle below her flat stomach seemed to glow with a golden fire.

She lifted her arms, beckoned.

With a loud groan, Orion fell into her arms, kissing her hungrily.

Her lips were warm and soft. She opened her mouth, her tongue snaking between his teeth. He let her enter, tasted her sweet saliva. Lifting her up, he carried her to the bed. With flying fingers, he opened his pants, pushed them past his hips. Then he stepped out of them and kicked them into a corner.

She lay there, her lovely naked body aglow. Her legs were wide open, inviting him. His phallus was swollen and almost painfully stiff and, with a groan, he pushed it deep into the waiting sheath of her pussy.

She cried out softly, meeting his thrusts. They thrashed around on the bed like two wild animals. He pushed and grunted and she whimpered and clawed at him as they worked their way to an incredible climax.

When it came, Azur clung to him, her legs wrapped around him, her heels digging into his buttocks. Her hot swollen labia rippled over his hard member and her inside muscles milked him until he was dry.

They separated, breathing heavily. He rolled onto his back and they lay without talking. After a while, she slipped from the bed. He watched, as she peeled off the thin transparent film. It pulled itself into a ball, thus becoming more visible. She put the little creature back into its container.

Orion felt the strange sensation lifting from his foggy brain and he shook his head to clear his thoughts.

Azur looked at him sheepishly. The irresistible glow that had surrounded her was gone. She was still pretty, but not as glamorous as she had seemed only moments ago.

"I apologize for seducing you like that," she said, her cheeks coloring again, "but it was necessary. We wanted to show you the power this little creature possesses and the pleasure it gives."

Orion smiled. "You are right. I rather enjoyed it, but you wouldn't have needed any help to seduce me. You're quite an attractive young woman, Azur, and very passionate."

"Thank you." She smiled shyly and hesitated. "I enjoyed what we did, too, but as handsome as you are, Mr. Orion, under ordinary circumstances I would not have coupled with you." She smiled and added, "At least not so fast."

"I understand, but I'm glad you did." His smile was warm and genuine. "Don't call me *Mr. Orion*, not after our intimate encounter. My name is Hektor."

She flushed and slipped into her dress, her dark lashes downcast.

He walked up to her and took her face between his hands. "Don't be ashamed." He kissed her gently. At first, she pushed at him, but then her arms snaked around his neck and she responded to his kiss.

Releasing her, he looked into her black eyes and wiped the teardrops from her cheek.

"I feel like a common whore," she whispered, staring at him.

"Don't," he said, stroking her hair. "I am not in the habit of hiring whores for my pleasure."

She gave him a warm smile and pressed herself against him. "Thank you, Hektor," she said, very gently pushing him away. "Go, get dressed now." She giggled suddenly. "In case some sex-starved female stumbles in here and tries to seduce you."

Laughing, he started to dress. Before he was finished, the door opened and a tall, thin man entered the room. He smiled at Azur and gave Orion a polite nod.

"I am Dr. Kirku. I see you've had your demonstration, Mr. Orion." He didn't smile when he said that and Orion refrained from making a remark. "Maybe now you understand why your help is needed."

Sitting on the edge of his bed, Orion looked without understanding at the other man. "That little creature has powerful emanations, Dr. Kirku, but frankly I don't quite know what is expected of me."

"The Mongo is an enigma to us, but it has been a way of life for the natives on Bakker's Planet since the beginning of intelligent life here. Without the Mongo, the humans may have never had a chance on this planet. And not just the humans. The natives are quite upset

23

with what is happening. Thousands of Mongos have been captured and removed from Bakker's Planet."

"My people are very angry," Azur interrupted. "If this continues, there won't be any Mongos left."

"She's right." Dr. Kirku nodded. "By the way, Azur's mother was a *Cylt*, a native. She has great interest in this. Without the Mongos, her mother's people and most of the other people native to this planet will eventually die out. And the Mongo? That little creature will disappear completely. We don't want that to happen."

* * * *

The white pebbles crushed under Orion's boots as he walked with Azur through the small garden. Overhead, the sun shone through the transparent dome, its bright light reflected in the still water of a small pond.

He looked past the shrubs and trees at the melting snow outside of the dome.

Azur saw him looking and pulled him down to sit beside her on a bench made from neatly piled up rocks.

"Soon the tribes will gather for the annual fertility rites, and my mother's people will have to go far to find enough Mongos for all the women who are of childbearing age."

"Have you ever taken part in one of those celebrations?" Orion asked.

She blushed slightly and shook her head. "No. Remember, I'm only half Cylt. My father, who was a scientist, took me away when I was still a child. I was raised on Orando. After my father died, I came back to Bakker's Planet, but I couldn't fit in with my mother's people. Their simple ways were not mine anymore. However, the bond is still there."

She took his hand into her slim one. "The Cylt and the other tribes are a proud people and they have a right to live. Much has been taken away from them already by outworlders. Their customs are slowly changing, but they will never survive without the Mango."

"What can I do to help?"

She smiled. "We know who you are, Hektor. You're an agent come to find out who's responsible for using Mongos as control brains in robots, which were manufactured by ELCOM."

"So much for my cover. Secrets sure travel fast here." Orion smiled ironically.

"Don't worry, only Kr. Kirku and I know."

"I'm not so sure about that. We were stopped by security men and they wanted to kill me. Someone tipped them off."

A loud beep interrupted their conversation and the voice of Dr. Kirku broke from Azur's wristband. "Azur, is Mr. Orion with you?"

"Yes, I am here." Orion bent a little to direct his voice into the built-in microphone. "Please, come to the main house. There is a call for you."

Orion and Azur walked quickly toward the big building at the north side of the garden. Dr. Kirku waited for them and indicated a large crystal cube, which showed the three-dimensional image of a familiar face.

"I see you have recovered." Azalee smiled, addressing Orion.

He grinned back. "Thanks to your friends here. But why didn't you stay?"

Her warm smile faded. "You were taken out of circulation for a while. I knew you were in good hands. There was no sense for me to hang around." She looked serious now. "You are a wanted man, Hektor. Security wants you badly. They know you are alive, and somehow they found out who you are. This call is probably monitored and by now, they know I've warned you. Get out of there fast."

Before Orion could reply, she broke the connection and, for a moment, he stared at the empty cube, a puzzled expression on his face. He turned to Azur. "You've heard," he said grimly. "I must move on. Problem is, I don't know where to go. I'm a stranger on this planet."

She nodded. "I'll come with you."

When Orion started to protest, she shook her head vehemently, looking at Dr. Kirku for help.

"She's right, Mr. Orion," the older man said. "As you've said, you are a stranger here. She can take you to a safe place. Don't forget, Azur was born on this planet. This is her home world."

"Alright," Orion agreed, reluctantly, realizing they were right. "Then let's get moving." He wondered how Security had found out about his hiding place, a nagging suspicion entered his mind, but he refused to believe it.

Hurriedly, they got ready. Orion's survival suit had been damaged beyond repair. Only his helmet and boots were intact.

Dressed in thick furs, Orion, Azur, and a tall, quiet man by the name of R'Mon, left the dome a short time later on the backs of stocky, longhaired animals. A fourth animal carried most of their

25

supplies.

They rode through a narrow valley, toward the mountains, which they reached after two hour's ride. The wind had picked up slightly and soon after, wet heavy snow began to fall. Even though the weather was unpleasant, they welcomed it, because the new snow would cover their tracks and make the search for them an almost impossible task.

Visibility was low and the going tough, but their steeds walked on doggedly, their heads down against the driving snow.

As bulky as the furs Orion and his companions wore, they kept them warm.

Orion cleaned the sleet from his visor and turned toward Azur, whose head was covered with a heavy fur cap. A flap of fur protected her face, only her eyes were visible, like two shiny black coals surrounded by a white furry ball.

"How long before we stop?" he called.

She shrugged and pointed at the tall figure in front of them. "When R'Mon decides, we'll stop."

"How does he know where he is going without a direction finder?"

He could sense her smile. "He knows. He may be only half-Ren, but he has the instincts of his mother's people. Trust him."

Orion shifted his weight on the animal's broad back. Not being used to riding, his backside began to get sore and his leg, although healed, seemed to throb with a dull pain. There was more snow on the ground now, as they climbed higher. Wet snow clung to their furs, making steed, and rider look like some giant, monstrous snow beast.

When they finally stopped to rest, it was almost dark. Orion slid off his steed and stomped his feet to get the circulation back into his cold toes and legs. His back ached and his buttocks seemed to be on fire. He walked around stiff-legged for a while and then he helped their guide to erect the tent.

It was large enough to accommodate all three of them, but R'Mon preferred to sleep outside with the animals.

Orion and Azur crawled into the tent and Azur adjusted the control for the heating unit built into the fabric of the tent. It didn't take long until the interior was comfortably warm.

They shed their furs and spread them on the floor. Then they sat cross-legged on the soft ground and listened to the howling of the raging wind outside. The tent rocked gently, as small pieces of ice hammered against the indestructible material.

"I feel sorry for R'Mon, who must surely be uncomfortable in this raging storm," Orion said.

Azur laughed. "You're wrong, Hektor. He'd be uncomfortable in this heat. Don't forget, he is a native to this planet, better adapted than even I am. I think his Ren part is stronger than his human part."

She opened a couple of plastic bags and handed one to Orion. He waited until the food began to heat up and then he consumed the steaming morsels with great gusto, realizing that he was quite hungry.

Afterwards both of them lay quietly for a while, resting their tired bodies.

When Azur sighed heavily, Orion turned his head to look at her profile. They had dimmed the small overhead light and her face lay in shadow. "Problems?" he asked in a low voice.

She smiled without looking at him. "Yesterday you told me that you found me attractive, even without the influence of the Mongo. Do you still?"

"Yes."

"Attractive enough to want to make love to me?"

"Yes."

She turned and switched off the light. He heard the soft rustling sounds as she slipped out of her clothes. When he knew she was ready, he put his hand on her naked breast, squeezing it gently.

She lay unmoving as he softly stroked her nude body. He felt her shiver and took her into his arms, his lips searching hers. Responding with slight reservation at first, she soon began to tremble in his embrace and pressed her nude, warm body against his, pushing her tongue into his mouth.

"It's not fair," she moaned. "You are still dressed."

With deft fingers, she opened his belt and pushed his trousers down, freeing his already erect penis. Then she tugged on his shirt. "I want you completely naked," she whispered. "I must feel your skin on mine."

He pulled his shirt over his head and then he rolled between her opening thighs. She took a hold of his straining phallus and rubbed it against her swollen labia. He felt the slippery wetness of her vagina and then, with a loud moan, she let go of him, and he slid effortlessly into her welcoming love channel.

This time he was in control and he eased his hard member in and out of her with slow, measured strokes. Soon she started to whimper and her breathing became ragged sobs. Her fingers dug into his buttocks and she met his every thrust as if she were trying to swallow his whole body.

He felt her climax several times and once he had to force his mouth over hers to keep her from screaming.

He kept it up for a long time, and when she finally whispered for him to stop, he shot his spermatic fluid into her hot vessel. She cried out and lifted her lower body off the ground, her belly working feverishly and her vulva pressing against him.

They stayed frozen like that until he finished gushing, and then, with a sigh, she relaxed and reluctantly released him.

"I guess the Mongo is not really necessary for me," she said after a while.

"That's what I tried to tell you, Love," he said gently and smiled. All this time, he had not even touched her mind. He was keeping that for another time.

Chapter Four

The wind had subsided by morning, but the snow was still falling. There was a lot of snow on the ground, and traveling would be slow and tedious.

R'Mon was already up and ready to leave, when Orion and Azur crawled out of the tent. If he knew what had transpired during the night, he didn't betray himself. He only grunted when Azur spoke to him, and then he began to pack up the tent and the rest of their belongings

The morning air was crisp and cold. Orion clamped the visor of his helmet shut, glad to have the built-in oxygen collector. Thankfully, he inhaled the warmed up oxygen enriched air.

Azur and R'Mon didn't seem to experience any discomfort breathing the freezing air. They didn't even cover their faces, since the wind had almost completely died down by the time they began to travel.

As they climbed higher, they found some places barren of snow and traveling became easier. For a long time they trekked along a high cliff on a narrow, natural road. On the other side of them, the ground was lost in haziness.

Orion wasn't exactly afraid of heights, but neither was he fond of them. He breathed easier when the ridge widened and leveled off.

"We've reached the highest point in our journey," Azur explained, "but not necessarily the hardest."

The animals were surefooted and the mountain seemed to be their natural domain, and yet, sometimes they stopped and refused to go on. It was on one of these stops when even R'Mon seemed uneasy.

He said something in his native language to Azur. When Orion inquired, she said, "Driggs."

"Driggs?" Orion repeated, not knowing what she meant.

"There is a pack of Driggs on our trail," she explained. "Carnivores, like most animals on this planet. They usually attack only lone travelers or animals, but sometimes they change their habits, especially when they're hungry. R'Mon spotted them a couple of hours ago. He was hoping they might give up following us."

"They're close," R'Mon said in Universal, for the first time looking directly at Orion.

Orion suppressed a smile. Obviously, the man waited for a reaction. Pushing up his visor, so the guide could see his face, Orion grinned. "I've fought wild animals before," he said.

"But not with your bare hands," R'Mon said, a slight sneer in his rumbling voice. "You star people don't go anywhere without your destructive weapons. I only use this." He unclipped the heavy bow he carried on his back and reached for an arrow. "I am a Ren," he said proudly. "Even though my father was not." His black eyes glinted and, with a sudden smooth movement, he swung around, the bow twanged and Orion heard the piercing howl of a wounded creature.

Before his eyes saw the white, hairy body lying in the snow behind them, his mind had already sensed the dying entity. Then he discovered three more creatures slinking close to the ground. They seemed to be a little over a meter in length and almost as tall at the shoulder when they stood up.

One was quite close and Orion could see the large and wide mouth with its double row of long, sharp teeth. A short crest ran from the ridged head along the back and ended at the base of the long, flat tail. Covered with white, short hair, the creature was nearly invisible against the snow.

"Watch their tails," warned Azur. "When they turn and lift them, throw yourself into the snow."

The nearest, the one Orion had been watching, came even closer and fell screaming, when an arrow pierced its thick hide.

Before R'Mon could nock another arrow, two more appeared too close for comfort. Orion fumbled in his furs for his energy gun and cursed when he encountered the empty holster under his arm.

Damn! Must have lost it at the last camping site.

While the third one fell under the guide's arrow, the last one turned and lifted its wide tail. Orion spied a short, narrow tube pointing in his direction and decided this was no time for heroism. He threw himself flat onto the ground, his face buried deep in the snow. When he heard the loud, wailing cry of a creature in agony, he followed his instinct and rolled away from the spot he lay on, just in time to get out of the way of his steed.

The screaming animal bucked and kicked, fell and began thrashing on the ground, legs tossing snow and loose rocks into the air.

Orion's hand touched something strapped to his side and he remembered the long knife. He drew it from its sheath, and when he saw the Drigg turn to point it's posterior at Azur, his hand whipped back and he buried the long blade just below the animal's lifted tail.

The tail flipped down and, after shuddering deeply, the Drigg lay still.

When Orion walked up to it to retrieve his knife, R'Mon stopped him. "Don't touch it, unless you want to burn your hand."

Orion looked at his steed. The beast had stopped kicking and lay on its side, unmoving. Half of its head was one mass of dark, blistering jelly.

"Acid," Azur said.

Shuddering, Orion looked at the remains of a dead Drigg lying in front of Azur. Its backside had been burned away. His eyes fastened on the small energy weapon in Azur's hand. She saw him looking and, with a shrug, handed it to him.

"I took it from you last night when you slept. I was going to give it back to you at a later time." Glancing at R'Mon, she said in a low voice, "I had my reasons. Don't ask."

"I guess I was wrong about you," R'Mon grumbled, staring down at the Drigg Orion had killed with his knife. "You are not entirely dependent on your superior weapons."

They stripped the gear from Orion's dead beast and divided it among the other three, the pack animal receiving the bulk of the load.

"We will take turns riding," R'Mon said to Orion. "I will walk ahead of you for now."

Since they were descending most of the time it was not too difficult, but as they climbed lower, the snow became deeper, making traveling tougher.

Orion welcomed evening. Even R'Mon didn't protest, when Azur suggested they stop and make camp.

Exhausted, Orion and Azur crawled into the warm interior of the tent, and both of them were happy just to lie and sleep. They slept naked to give their clothing a chance to dry out.

It was near morning, when tender hands stroking his chest, his stomach, and finally fumbling between his legs woke him. He kept his eyes closed as Azur straddled him. Her trembling hands grasped his erect phallus and moved the tip back and forth at the entrance of her already moist vagina. Finally, with a deep sigh, she let go and eased herself down, letting the soft walls of her sheath closing tightly around his straining member.

Slightly opening his eyes, he watched her face as she rode him fiercely. Her large breasts were taut and the nipples stood out firm and erect. He wanted to touch them, but he kept his hands to himself, leaving her in control.

He reached out with his mind and, slowly, he joined their minds together. She didn't know what was happening, but when she reached her orgasm, her eyes were unfocused and her lovely face a contorted mask. She whimpered and clawed at him, pushing down faster and faster. Her mouth opened to let out a silent scream as waves and waves of pleasure washed through her.

Orion's own climax had been building up, and when they both reached the peak, his hands clamped around her hips and held her still.

Crying out hoarsely, he erupted. When it was over, she collapsed on top of him, her arms and legs limp on either side of him, her breath coming in great gasps. Finally, her breathing became normal, and she kissed him gently. "I hope you're not angry," she whispered.

He chuckled, stroking her soft buttocks. "Why should I be angry? I was only raped."

Laughing, she playfully nibbled his ear, her black hair like a veil over his face. He blew at it and put his arms around her.

She felt good in his arms and, with a satisfied sigh, he drifted back to sleep.

* * * *

He awoke with a strong feeling of dread. Azure had slipped to one side, but her legs were still clamped around him.

Outside, an animal screamed, and then he heard a terrifying roar. Wide-awake now, he pushed Azur off him. Opening her eyes, she yawned and stretched her lithe body. She froze as a second roar broke the silence. Orion saw her open mouth, knew she was talking, but the ripping noise of something tearing drowned out her voice. Then the sky opened up above them.

As the tent collapsed, Orion grabbed the young woman and rolled with her away from the large shadow looming over them.

The cold snow was a searing pain on his naked skin, but he shut it out, aware only of the immediate danger. Whatever it was that had ripped the supposedly indestructible material of the tent was huge. He only perceived giant tusks and gleaming talons.

All around them, the snow was red with blood. One of their beasts lay unmoving, its throat ripped open and its entrails covering the snow. R'Mon crouched behind the slain beast, his bow in his hand.

Useless against the monstrosity blotting out the sky above.

"A *Lepra-Dragon*," Azur cried. "We are surely lost!"

The colossal beast snarled and eyed the pitiful humans. Orion estimated it to be at least four meters tall and twice as long, all muscle, bone and teeth. Shaggy coarse hair covered its huge body and it moved on six powerful legs, frighteningly faster than an animal this size should be able to move.

Naked and weaponless, Orion felt small and vulnerable.

"Get back!" R'Mon called to Orion. "I'll try to hold it as long as I can."

Orion laughed grimly. "Don't be a fool, R'Mon."

The arrow in the guide's bow was no more than a toothpick against this ferocious beast.

The guide pulled back the bowstring and shot an arrow into the open maw of the Lepra-Dragon. The animal shook its giant head, roaring and spitting, but otherwise unhurt. It advanced toward R'Mon, and he barely managed to evade the ripping claws.

Orion watched it sink its teeth into the dead pack animal, and then he looked at the collapsed tent. There was only one way to get out of this situation alive.

On his belly, he crept slowly toward the tent and searched for the power pack. He found it, ripped it loose, and opened the control panel. His fingers were beginning to get numb, making it difficult to pry open the service cover. He had done this before, but he knew it was dangerous. Timing was most important or they could all wind up blown to tiny pieces.

Then he searched for his small energy gun, found it and set it to a narrow, weak beam. Very carefully and taking time he didn't have, he fused together sections of the power pack's control unit.

He heard Azur's warning scream and looked up right into a double row of gleaming, dagger-like teeth.

This was almost better than he had hoped. When the jaws opened wider, he threw the rigged power pack into the yawning throat. At the same time, he threw himself backwards.

While he rolled away, he heard a dull explosion, and then the snow around him turned red and mushy as blood, fragments of bone, hair, and bloody chunks of meat rained from the sky.

He lifted his head to look for Azur. She was already running for the tent and searching for her clothes.

Only now, he became aware of the severe cold and his shaking body. He joined her in her search. Blood and gore covered both of them and, after wiping it off with snow, they wrapped the furs around their frozen bodies.

Orion slipped into his boots and activated the built-in heating grid. Soon almost painful warmth started moving back into his toes and feet.

Shivering, Azur stared at the ruined remnants of their tent. "It seems our cozy nights are a thing of the past," she said, smiling sadly. "Just when I was beginning to get used to them. The nights will be cold from now on."

Putting his arms around her and pulling her close, he held her for a moment. "We're alive. That's all that counts. We'll worry about other things when we have to." He let go of her and looked for R'Mon.

The guide stood not far away, watching them. "We must move on as quickly as possible," he said. "This meat will attract many scavengers, and their hunters will not be far away."

Orion knew R'Mon was right and he nodded. Then he helped the guide to load their gear and most of the stuff they managed to salvage on the backs of the remaining two animals. Without breakfast, they started the journey, but after a couple of hours, they stopped to rest and eat.

While they ate, Orion noticed R'Mon's eyes flicker toward him several times.

"I don't like your destroying weapons," the guide said suddenly, "however, without your quick thinking and your knowledge we would fill the Lepra's belly now."

Orion nodded and grinned. "I guess a little know-how is of some advantage in certain situations."

"And courage," R'Mon said, his black eyes full on Orion's face. "You have great courage, starman." He stood up and walked away to feed the animals some of his food concentrates.

Seeing Orion's perplexed expression, Azur laughed, but her dark eyes were serious. "He gave you a compliment, Hektor. That's all you're going to hear from him about the encounter with the Lepra-Dragon." She bent forward and looked at him, a mystic smile on her face. "Don't worry, your feat won't be forgotten. I'll tell our son all about his father, the great warrior, who slew the giant Snow-Beast."

"What do you mean by *our son*? We don't have a son."

She giggled and patted her stomach. "Oh, yes, we do. I can feel it."

"Don't be silly. There hasn't been enough time." He didn't like the direction this conversation was taking. The last things he needed were complications.

Azur came close, pulled down his head and kissed him on the lips. "Women know more about these things than men." She touched his cheek. "I won't tie you down, if that's what you fear. It was my choice. I wanted it this way. It happened the first time we made love, when I used the Mongo. You not only fathered a son, you also helped to create another generation of Mongos."

"I'm thrilled," Orion said.

They rested every two hours. In the late afternoon, they had descended into a deep gorge and the traveling became easier. Only patches of snow covered the ground, but a cold icy wind blew through the ravine and Orion pulled the visor over his face.

Night came quickly and, after a quick meal of a handful of tasteless food concentrates, Orion lay down on the hard ground. He felt grimy and uncomfortable inside his furs, and the remnants of blood and gore on his skin from the exploding Lepra-Dragon made him itch. He longed for a long soaking in a tub filled with hot water.

Azur, who had gone to find some privacy, came back from the shadows and dropped down beside him. Smiling, she lifted her lips for his kiss and snuggled into his arms. She sniffed, and Orion could see her wrinkled nose in the semi-darkness.

"I think we both need a bath," she murmured.

He was too tired to answer and just nodded.

* * * *

Darkness descended upon them and the pale light of the full moon shone on the fur covered entwined bodies of Azur and her alien lover. R'Mon was leaning against the stocky body of one of the snorting animals, his long bow within reach. He watched the sleeping pair quietly for a while, a thoughtful expression on his usually stoic face.

He had listened the nights before to their violent lovemaking and he felt a stab of jealousy and envy toward the starman. The part of him that was not of this planet made him different from the men of his mother's tribe. He had suppressed it and tried to tell himself he was a full-blooded *Ren,* but he knew otherwise.

Listening to their ecstatic moaning and groaning, seeing Azur's naked body in the snow, had caused a strange pounding and desire in his loins…even in the face of death.

The natives of this planet didn't really know the meaning of love between a man and a woman. Only at the *Time of the Mongo*, a woman would seek out a man, and he became nothing more than a wild animal under the hypnotic spell of a small insignificant creature. He'd couple with any woman of childbearing age. She could be young, old, fat, beautiful or ugly, it didn't matter, as long as she satisfied that urge inside him and took that appendix between his legs, which suddenly had become a rigid, unyielding pole, into her belly.

He remembered the last fertility celebration he had taken part in, but the memory was hazy and dreamlike.

His naked sweating body lying on top of yielding, warm flesh, his frenzied stabbing between two opening and closing thighs. The hot, slippery wetness as his pole slid into hot incredible softness. The burning fire rushing through his body when his spermatic fluid filled the vessel beneath him.

Sometimes he felt strange urges when looking at the nude bodies of bathing young girls, their strutting round breasts, their round buttocks, the thick bushy triangles below their bellies.

He had watched them as sometimes they touched each other intimately; saw their slim hands running over naked skin, lingering on breasts, thighs, and fingers disappearing between squeezing thighs. The way they kissed. He had seen, and the rod between his legs had stirred, grown in size.

These feelings were wrong, so he had been told, not normal, but living with the outworlders had taught him differently.

This starman named Orion, he was a man. A warrior. Despite his sexual urges.

I am a Ren, but part of me belongs to the world my father came from. My father had been a proud and strong man, a warrior in his own right.

As the moon traveled on past the mountain that shadowed the gorge, R'Mon fell into an uneasy and troubled slumber.

Chapter Five

By noon the next day, they came to the entrance of a large cave.

"We'll enter the mountain here," R'Mon said. "From here on we'll be safe."

The tunnel they followed was narrow and low at first, but widened as they traveled deeper into the interior. A soft light from the walls and ceiling illuminated the tunnel, and after examining it closer, Orion realized it was some kind of lichen growing on the moist surface. The light seemed to get brighter as they traveled on.

Passing many openings to other tunnels, they stayed in the main tunnel. The ground seemed well traveled, and once they were met by a group of natives stepping out of one of the side tunnels, four men, carrying the carcasses of large, rodent-like animals on their shoulders.

The strangers halted when they saw the three, dropped their burden, and reached for the bows they had strapped across their backs. R'Mon called to them and they relaxed, lifted a hand with the fingers spread wide, then they picked up the carcasses and disappeared into another tunnel.

"They belong to the P'tar tribe," R'Mon explained. "Hunters coming back from a successful hunt."

The temperature had begun to rise steadily and they took off their furs, bundled them up to carry over their shoulders. Once, they stopped to rest and take some nourishment.

While they sat, Orion seemed to hear the faint gurgling sound of running water and wondered what lay ahead.

The sound grew louder and, after traveling for another twenty minutes or so, the tunnel suddenly widened into a large cavern. A wide river split it almost in half. The narrow, natural bridge spanning the river looked treacherous, but turned out to be wider and safer than Orion had expected when he first saw it.

Their animals were somewhat reluctant, but after some coaxing from R'Mon, they stepped onto the narrow path to follow him.

Orion and Azur walked slowly behind them. The water looked black and murky in the dim, somewhat eerie light. It moved quite swiftly along, bubbling and gurgling as it flowed around obstacles breaking through the water's surface.

Orion saw more tunnel openings in the rough walls of the cavern, but once they safely reached the other side of the bridge, they traveled along the bank of the underground river.

They ran into another party of hunters. This time, one of them clasped R'Mon's arm and slapped his shoulder enthusiastically. They didn't pay much attention to Azur, but looked at Orion with critical and watchful eyes.

"They are from my tribe," R'Mon said. He indicated the man who had so elatedly greeted him. "This is one of my mother's sons. He is a true Ren, born before my father claimed my mother for his own, as is the custom on his home world."

Not quite knowing what the guide meant, Orion did understand that there was a strong bond between these two men, having the same mother. He nodded toward the other man. "I am honored to know you, brother of R'Mon," he said in Universal.

The man just scowled, but after R'Mon translated and added a few more comments of his own, he broke into a wide grin and lifted his right fist. Then he said something in his native tongue.

"He is proud to know you also," R'Mon explained. "He says 'A man who kills a Snow-Beast must be a great warrior, even if he walks around in strange and ugly clothing'."

"Thanks for the compliment, I guess," Orion muttered. Behind him, he heard Azur suppress a giggle. "He thinks you look like a *Kribb*," she said in a low voice.

"What's a *Kribb*?"

She giggled again, touching his helmet. "A rodent that likes to wear the empty shell of a *Burr*-egg on its head."

Orion sighed, removed the helmet, and hung it from his belt. The other men had been watching him, seemingly waiting for his reaction, but he detected no malice in their behavior. Smiling, he pointed to his head. "Is this better?" he asked, but they just shook their heads and smiled.

After speaking a few more words to R'Mon, they stepped into one of the tunnels.

Orion checked the timepiece on his wrist. It was night outside, but in here, there was eternal twilight. Traveling on, they walked on the worn path running along the river's edge.

The cavern had gradually become a wide tunnel, with the ceiling dipping so low at times that they had to walk uncomfortably stooped over. Sometimes Orion heard splashes in the water below, evidence of some kind of life form inhabiting the river. After another good hour, the tunnel became wider and the ceiling rose, until it became hazy in the darkness above their heads. Suddenly, a number of men with large bows ready in their hands appeared from dark niches and barred their way.

Again, R'Mon spoke to them and, after a few tense moments, they let the three travelers pass. Orion sensed the presence of people and, slightly opening his mind, he sent out searching thought-tendrils.

He discovered many people ahead, most of them asleep.

R'Mon led them through the cavern until they came to a number of dark holes in the wall. Outside, half a dozen armed men sat or leaned against large boulders. They looked sleepily at the three intruders, trusting the sentries who had let them pass.

R'Mon addressed one of the men, speaking in a subdued tone. The guard gestured to a small cave and R'Mon waved to Orion and Azur, indicating they should follow him.

They entered the cave mouth and Orion discovered that it was actually another tunnel with more openings on both sides. They stepped through one of these openings into a small cave. Only a few scattered patches of lichen grew on the ceiling, illuminating the interior with a faint light.

Soft furs covered the floor. Orion counted five small sleeping bodies huddled together in one corner. Two more bodies lay on the other side, two females; he could see their bare breasts. One of them had her hand touching the other one's belly, her fingers curled in the thick bush between her slightly parted legs.

The guide pointed into an empty corner, and then he lay down beside the smaller sleepers. Azur pulled Orion down into the furs and cuddled up against him.

Orion was very tired, but he lay awake for some time, listening to Azur's gentle breathing beside him. It was warm inside the cave and he detected a slightly musky odor in the air. He fought the impulse to cover his head with his helmet so he could breathe filtered oxygen-enriched air.

His body finally demanded payment and he drifted off into a deep sleep. There was safety here, and not until now had he realized how tired he really was. Outside, he had to be alert at all times, even when sleeping, but in here, he could let down his guard, and give his body and mind the rest they craved and deserved.

* * * *

It was the *Time of the Mongo*. The following nights would be filled with laughter and celebrating. The women had been successful in their search for Mongos. All the girls who were of age would be filled with the seed, and the Mongos would be released, their tendrils saturated with drops of spermatic fluid, their survival insured.

Orion sensed the excitement hovering over the tribe.

The young men and girls, who would be taking part in the celebration for the first time, were anxious and just a little bit afraid. Older friends and siblings, who had gone through the ceremonies already, told all kinds of stories. Especially the men.

There was one tale going around how one man with an enormous pole had been attacked by a group of women, crazy and out of control. After he had put his organ into the bellies of ten of them, he collapsed from exhaustion. The screaming women had finally ripped out his still rigid and throbbing member, demanding satisfaction.

The rigid piece of flesh was passed from woman to woman and, apparently, they were still using it secretly at night, when the men were asleep.

Orion smiled when one of the young men told him the story and shyly asked if by chance Orion was well endowed. Should this be the case, he would be well advised to keep it out of sight.

The next day was filled with hustle and bustle, as the tribe got ready for the night. The men were busy collecting fungus and hunting the rodent-like *Sleem,* while the women prepared the food. The aroma of boiling stew rose from large posts and tantalized the noses, adding to the excitement.

Most of the activities were going on in the great cavern. Diffused daylight streamed in through large openings in the ceiling, which was nearly out of sight. It was strong enough to change the gloomy twilight into pleasant brightness.

A large patch of yellow sand along the river's edge created a beautiful beach. Orion sat on a boulder and watched the smaller children splashing in the water and roll in the soft sand.

Azur had joined the women to help with the preparations. He would have liked to travel on, but she told him it was out of the question. They had to stay until the festivities were over, then a member of the tribe would guide them on through the mountain.

He had no concrete idea where they were headed. For now, it was important to stay out of sight, hidden away from the searching security men. For some reason they wanted him dead, proof enough that someone felt vulnerable and didn't want him to find out who was behind the fiasco on Apex.

Azur and Dr. Kirku had pleaded for his help in finding out who was responsible for the capture and disappearance of the Mongo. There wasn't much he could do hiding inside a mountain.

When darkness came, small fires were blazing throughout the cavern, with the men sitting around them, eating and drinking.

The women had gone into the caves to prepare themselves.

Orion felt somewhat out of place among the decorated men. They had put on beautifully woven shirts and soft leather kilts. On their heads, they wore headgear made from the bones of animals. Some of them wore bracelets around their arms and legs, amulets around their necks.

Others had painted their bodies with bright designs. All were laughing and talking loud, bragging about successful hunts and encounters with dangerous beasts. The brew from the tall earthenware containers was flowing freely and put everyone into a good mood.

Occasionally some of them, especially the younger ones, would glance toward the caves and then quickly look away, afraid to show their anxiety.

A tall native, his naked upper body decorated with swirling colors, crouched down beside Orion.

It was R'Mon.

He looked at the mug in Orion's hand and smiled. "Be careful with that. It is very strong and it will dull your senses. I don't believe you need it to overcome any fears, like some of the others."

Detecting a somewhat bitter, but also envious undertone in the guide's friendly advice, Orion shook his head and looked at the other man. "I am a bit apprehensive, R'Mon, because I don't know what to expect. I am not even certain if I have the right to take part in this celebration."

R'Mon was silent for a moment, pondering what Orion had said. His eyes stared into the fire, his face an unreadable mask. Suddenly, he smiled. "You have as much right as I have, starman. Some fresh blood might be good for the tribe. You are a brave warrior. Maybe the gods led you here to enhance the tribe's strength and courage."

Orion didn't have a chance to answer. He became aware of the sudden silence, and then from the caves came a rhythmic drumming sound. Faint at first, then becoming louder as the tempo accelerated.

The men picked up the rhythm and started to sway, clapping their hands to the beat of the drums. As the drums came to a thundering crescendo, the women appeared. They were naked, their painted bodies glistening in the flickering light of the fires.

While most of the men were decorated with a multitude of colors, each woman had chosen only one color. Some of them shone with an iridescent blue, some were painted red, some white, others black or green.

The thunder of the drums had been replaced by the wailing sounds of some musical instrument.

Orion sat silent and rigid, like all the other men, watching the swaying bodies of the women coming closer.

At first, he contributed it to the strong brew he had consumed. His head seemed to swim in a foggy environment and he felt a strange detachment from his surroundings. He could have sworn he had seen some fat and old women in the crowd of swaying bodies and yet, as the women came closer, he was stricken by their great beauty, admired their perfect bodies, their lovely breasts, their glistening thighs.

He couldn't keep his eyes away from the pulsing triangle below their bellies. The pounding in his loins became stronger as he watched one of those angelic figures single him out.

Her lovely body glowed bright blue and only the nipples of her perfect breasts were untouched by paint. She smiled, lifted her arms and, with a groan, he sank into her embrace, his mouth searching her erect brown nipples. He began sucking on them like a newborn baby.

Her hands opened his pants, pushed them down and found his straining member.

He was not aware of the other men and women and didn't see their entwined bodies, didn't hear their ecstatic moans and screams. The only thing he saw and felt, was the beautiful goddess in his arms.

They sank to the floor and, while his lips crushed hers and her tongue snaked into his mouth, his throbbing penis glided into her moist cleft, guided by her eager hands. Her fingers dug into his buttocks and her legs lifted up to let him plunge his hard member deep into her sucking sheath.

Every time he pushed into her, she gave a little scream, but her hands kept pulling him to her. Her pussy couldn't get enough of him. The tight soft walls pulsed around his hard penis and demanded the release of his pent up desire.

When his climax came, it was like roaring thunder.

Suddenly he realized he was no longer in the arms of the blue love goddess. His hands were clamped around a pair of red-painted hips and he was pounding his lower body against two lovely shaped buttocks.

He couldn't see the kneeling woman's face, but judging from the shape of her body it couldn't be anything but beautiful.

She arched her back and met each of his strokes with a powerful push backwards, engulfing his painfully erect penis with her tight, slippery cunt. He erupted again, spilling his seed into her. She quivered against him, her fingers raking the ground, her mouth emitting tiny mewling sounds. When he pulled out of her, she sank to the ground, but he wasn't given any time to relax.

Two hands pushed him backwards and a yellow-painted woman straddled him, the lips of her pulsing love-sheath closing greedily around his throbbing mast. She rode him as if he were a wild beast that needed taming, her beautiful face upturned and contorted by the rapturous pleasure she experienced.

His hands grabbed her bobbing swollen breasts, his fingers dug deep into the soft flesh.

Suddenly, his mind seemed to clear a little and he became aware of himself and his surroundings. He knew now what was happening and he tried to gain control. His thoughts reached out and touched the primitive mind of the Mongo. He was only partially successful to neutralize the hypnotic emanations.

The female above him was just a girl, but still quite lovely. This was probably the first time she took part in the celebration.

Her eyes were unfocused and she moved erratically, her shapely bottom gyrating around his shaft. His hands slid down to her hips and gently he steadied her movements, lifted her up and down slowly and steadily.

At first, she resisted, but then she followed his guiding hands. Carefully, he entered her mind and erected a barrier against the influence of the Mongo.

Coming out of her trance, she stopped moving and her eyes focused on his face. Then she looked down to where their bodies where joined and gasped. "You are the stranger from the stars. What are you doing to me?" she cried out in Universal.

Looking around, she saw the other couples locked together and writhing on the ground.

"The *Night of the Mongo*," she said, wondering. "What has happened? Why has the spell left me?"

He pulled her down and kissed her gently. Her soft breasts pressed against his hard chest and he held her tightly for a moment. "This is the way it should really be," he murmured into her ear. She trembled in his arms and he sensed her uneasiness.

"It is wrong," she whispered.

"No," he said, "just different. Relax and let your body follow its instincts." He helped her along, let his hands travel along her body, gently massaging her soft round buttocks. Then he rolled her onto her back and, with slow measured strokes, he moved between her widely spread thighs.

Soon she was bucking wildly, her buttocks lifting off the ground to meet his thrusts. After a series of orgasms, she clung to him, her legs wrapped around his. "I didn't know this could be so wonderful," she gasped. "I wish I could go on forever, but if we don't stop soon, I think I'm going to faint."

He smiled and, with a few deep thrusts, he came to another shattering climax. The girl whimpered softly, throwing her head from side to side, clawing at his back. Then she sighed and her body relaxed.

"Had I known this is so pleasurable, I would have done it a long time ago with the boys at the Outworlder School."

"You went to an Outworlder School?" Orion asked.

She nodded. Now he understood why she spoke Universal so fluently. He wanted to ask more questions, but somebody grabbed him, pushed him down, and then a fat, black-painted woman mounted him. Her huge breasts flopped up and down as she bounced on top of him.

He sighed and gave up his control on the Mongo spell. Suddenly, a young, shapely woman gyrated slowly in his lap, smiling sweetly at him. Through the powerful influence of the Mongo, his penis had swollen to monstrous proportions again and he yielded to the terrible urge that drove his body.

A small part of his mind knew that he was still coupling with the fat woman, but he didn't care. To him she was the most beautiful woman in the universe and he drove his throbbing member into her pulsing love-box, his grunts, and groans blending with her ecstatic cries.

Chapter Six

He didn't know how long he slept. He must have passed out during the long night. When he awoke, he found himself sprawling naked amidst a group of snoring, painted bodies. Looking around, he saw some of them moving and sitting up.

There were only men.

All the women were gone.

His hand went to his head. "What an experience," he murmured. The memory of the night was slightly blurred, but he must have made love to a dozen or so women during the celebration, and climaxed with each one of them. How his body had found the strength, he couldn't even guess.

With weak legs, he stumbled to one of the large pots hanging over a small mountain of cold ashes and looked inside. His fingers trembled slightly when he scooped some leftover stew from the bottom. It was cold and tasted slightly burned, and gamy, but he wolfed it down. Then he found a pitcher half filled with the strong brew and emptied it.

"You must have had a real good time last night," said a chuckling voice beside him. He jumped, cursing loudly.

My body reserves must really be down. Usually nobody could approach me this close without me knowing it.

"I guess I did." He grinned at Azur, a little sheepishly. She was as naked as he was.

She laughed and hugged him. "Don't feel guilty, lover. I was not exactly idle. For me this was also the first time to take part in the fertility celebration." She gave him an impish smile. "Not that it was necessary for me."

Orion cringed silently. He still couldn't get used to her way of thinking. She didn't seem to mind sharing him with other women, but then he remembered that her tribe didn't really have any family ties. Her native language didn't even know the words father, wife, husband, or lover.

"I think I need a bath," he said.

She wrinkled her pert nose. "You're right. You do."

She took his hand and pulled him with her. "Come on, we'll go swimming together. I'm also in need of a bath."

They walked down to the small beach, where a few natives, men and women, were already frolicking nude in the somewhat murky water. Azur jumped into the water and splashed him. He plunged in after her. It was cold but refreshing.

She swam surprisingly well and he followed her down the river, past an outcropping of rocks. When they were out of sight of the others, she swam toward shore and climbed on top of the rocks, where she sat, smiling alluringly at him. She opened her arms and said, "Come."

Orion looked at her naked lovely form. Drops of water clung to her coppery skin, ran down between her up-tilted breasts, across her stomach to the black thick triangle between her slightly open legs.

"Come," she said again, and then she lay back against the rock.

He was panting when he reached her and, with a hoarse cry, he drove his erect penis into her. Through the whole time they made love, she was smiling, her black eyes shiny, and never leaving his face.

His mind reached for hers and he sensed a strange happiness inside her. When he climaxed, she clawed at him and closed her eyes. Moaning softly, she held him until he was spent.

When his breathing finally returned to normal, he sat up and stared at her as she lay giggling on the rock.

"When I saw you eat and drink this morning I knew you'd be ready for me," she said, still giggling.

"I think I'm beginning to understand. It's in the food."

She nodded. "It's a fungus. It is eaten only on special occasions. Sometimes, when the men go on a long and dangerous hunt, they eat from it. Besides providing strength and endurance, it takes away the fear of the unknown. However, as with many things, it can be habit forming."

"In other words, it's a drug."

"You can call it that." She stretched her young trim body, moving sensuously on the dark rock. "I love you, you know," she said suddenly. Even the twilight could not hide the moisture in her eyes.

He touched her wet cheek. "I love you, too," he said gently, "but please don't get hung up on me. We live in two different worlds, you and I."

She nodded and smiled. "I know, my love, I know." She clung to him. "It is such a new and strange experience for me. You are like no other man I ever met. I have one consolation; even if I can't have you, your son will always keep your memory alive."

"My son," he murmured. "How can you be so damn sure?"

Her fingers trailed down his broad chest. She smiled happily, as she regarded his brooding face. "I told you before, I know. I'll be a good mother, don't worry. He'll be a very special child."

I know he will be, and that's what worries me.

Although he'd be his firstborn, he would not be a carrier. Had he, Orion, at the time of the baby's conception chosen to trigger the necessary command, the genes of his son would have carried with them the *Ancient Memory*. As it was, he would only be gifted with exceptional abilities. Growing up without the right guidance, they might not be a blessing but a curse.

He shrugged mentally. Maybe Azur was wrong about being pregnant; maybe she just imagined it. How could she even know after only a few days? However, should she be right, he'd have to check up on the progress of his son from time to time. He'd have to make certain the boy grew up in a favorable environment.

Hew bent and kissed Azur's smiling lips. "Everything will be all right. I will make sure of that," he told her. "Come on, let's swim back now. I'd like to move on, get out of these caves. I still have a mission to carry out."

Azur reached for his hand, letting him pull her up. She smiled strangely. "I imagine you put your seed into many women last night," she said.

He shrugged, somewhat embarrassed. "A few, I guess. What does it matter?"

"That's good. Our son won't be alone then. He'll have many brothers and sisters."

"Alone?" he asked, a sudden knowledge dawning. In all probability, he had fathered at least a dozen children last night. He remembered R'Mon's words.

Some fresh blood might be good for the tribe.

Orion wasn't sure if that was necessarily the truth. This new blood would bring many changes to the tribe in the years ahead.

He plunged into the cool water to clear his head, cursing himself for being so careless.

When the came back to the large cavern, they found R'Mon searching for them. He was accompanied by two young men.

"This is Drom and this one here is M'Tay." He pointed at the taller and older of the two. "M'Tay speaks your language. They will lead you the rest of the way."

Orion clasped R'Mon's hand. "Thank you for your help, friend. Maybe some day our paths will cross again and I can repay the debt."

R'Mon smiled, his white teeth a stark contrast in his dark face. "I've learned much from you, starman. I was honored to guide you here. I have finally realized that you came here to help my people and I wish you success...friend."

Orion watched the tall man walk away, proud and so sure of himself...on the outside, but he had read the turmoil in the other man's mind. There was much he still needed to sort out. He had to decide what he wanted to be...a Ren, who followed the laws of his tribe or a citizen of Bakker's Planet, shrug off old ties and learn the new ways of the star people, the ways of his father.

"Good luck," Orion said quietly. "I think you'll do the right thing."

Azur looked at him, questions in her eyes.

He shrugged. "It's nothing. Just thinking out loud."

* * * *

The current of the underground river was slow, but strong enough to push their small boat ahead at a steady, moderate speed.

The boat was a strange contraption, made from the husk of a *Wilm*, a wormlike creature that lived in the underground caverns. Shaped and dried, the tough shell was lightweight, but extremely strong. It provided plenty of room inside for the four travelers and their possessions.

Drom, the younger of the two, sat silently in the front, occasionally dipping a paddle into the water to keep them on course. The other one, M'Tay, sat facing Orion. "What is your home world like, Hektor?"

Orion smiled. He had taken an instant liking to the youth with the big, open smile and a million questions.

"It's been many years since I left the world I was born on. A medium sized planet, the fourth of seven circling a sun called Sirius. Very far from here, at the edge of the Galaxy. Not far from a small planet known as Earth or Terra, the center of the human empire. My ancestors came from there."

"What is this Earth like?"

"Earth is an overcrowded world, where huge cities sprawl across once fertile land, with buildings reaching into the sky. Buildings as large as cities, where people live like ants. Domed cities in the oceans, because they ran out of space on the available land. No more room for animals, only people. The air is polluted, the planet's resources depleted because nobody cared when greedy companies cut down the forests and jungles and robbed the planet of valuable non-renewable minerals and metals. You wouldn't like it."

"What about your own home world?"

"Heading the same way. Too close to Earth."

"Is that why you left?"

Orion shrugged. "The nature of my work takes me to many different worlds. I'm not tied to one anymore."

"It must be very exciting to travel across the emptiness of space and to see the stars from the outside." M'Tay had a dreamy look on his face. "I used to look at the big starships when they lifted into the sky to disappear among the clouds, and I imagined myself to be one of the travelers, to jump from one world to another, to loose myself among all those lights, which are called stars, never to come back here again."

"You don't like it here?" Orion asked.

It took a moment for the young man to come back to reality. His eyes focused on Orion. "This is my home," he said, spreading his arms. "My people have lived in these caves for a long time, maybe too long. I was among the chosen to live in one of the surface cities, to learn about the star people. I have learned much. I have learned that there are places where men walk the surface of their world without heavy clothing, where the air is warm and the sun shines bright. Where you can pick sweet fruit from tall, straight plants called trees. Where there are no large and dangerous animals. I want to see those places."

His eyes looked into Orion's. "I was told about a world called Eden, where man and beast live side by side, like brothers."

"You may be disappointed, son," Orion said, thoughtfully. "There is a snake in every garden."

"I don't understand, Hektor."

Orion shook his head, smiling. "An old saying it would take too long to explain. What it means is, wherever you live, it always looks better someplace else." He chuckled. "Another old saying goes like this: The grass is always greener on the other side."

Something stirred deep inside him. Fragments of almost forgotten memories drifted into his consciousness, memories from long ago, impressed into his human genes by that part of his mind that was alien.

He remembered another time, another galaxy. The flight from the evil Hunters who were bent on destroying all life that was not like them.

The Hunters. The shape shifters.

The snake in the garden.

He looked up into the questing eyes of the youth, pushing the memories back where they belonged. "Maybe some day you'll get a chance to see your dreams come true."

"How about now?" M'Tay's voice sounded urgent. "Let me come with you all the way. I could assist you in your work, whatever it is you do. I learn fast."

"I'm sorry, M'Tay. I wish I could help you." Orion grabbed the young man's shoulder. "But I will talk with some influential people I know and I'm sure they will give you all the assistance you need." He looked at the young woman sitting beside him. "Maybe Azur will put in a good word for you," he said, smiling.

She nodded, squeezing Orion's hand. M'Tay gave Azur a thoughtful look, and then he shrugged. "Much good it will do. She's a Cylt."

"Only half of me," Azure said.

"What's the difference? Most of the outworlders think we are stupid, nothing but a bunch of primitive savages who run around naked in dark underground tunnels, chasing Mongos for our fertility rites," the youth blurted out, sounding bitter and disappointed. "I am proud to be a Ren, but only another Ren appreciates that fact. I want to go where people treat me as an equal man."

"Prejudice is not limited to your world, M'Tay," Orion said. "Humanity has not progressed very far in that respect."

M'Tay didn't answer. He sat silent and sulking, staring into the dark water. Orion didn't mind. He was still tired and put his head on Azur's shoulder.

Snuggling against him, she whispered, "Tired?"

He nodded, closing his eyes. The gently motion of the little craft lulled him into sleep. His senses had not detected any immediate danger. He didn't know what lay ahead and he was thankful for the chance to rest his body.

He slept. He dreamed.

She stood there, smiling. Her beautiful face was radiant with the news she had to tell him.

"I am pregnant," she said. "We will have a son."

"A son?" he asked. "My son?"

Her silvery laughter mocked him a little, and then she pouted. "Are you implying I was unfaithful?"

He took her into his arms. She was naked, his hand touched her belly, could almost feel the beat of new life inside her.

"My son," he repeated. The son he had chosen to be the carrier of the Ancient Memory.

She stepped out of his embrace, stepped back and struck a pose. "Do you still find me attractive?"

He studied her rounded buttocks, her slender legs, the curve of her hip, her smooth belly, her full high breasts. She stood proudly, her red lips slightly parted, knowing how he enjoyed looking at her body, letting him feast his eyes and at the same time getting her own pleasure out of his admiration and love for her.

"I love you," he said, his mind reaching out for hers. Her own mind responded to the mind touch, opened to let him enter. She saw herself with his eyes as he saw himself through hers.

She sank to the ground, parted her legs, beckoned with her arms.

"Come," she called.

He couldn't. Between them, a gulf had suddenly split the ground. He saw her struggling in the arms of two men. No...not men. They had long reptilian heads.

Snakes.

Hunters!

Hissing and laughing, they laid her on top of an altar. The ancient stone was stained dark, and his mind reeled from the horror of this place. Above him, the giant stone image of the snake god glared at him. He saw the evil flicker of light in the staring eyes, the flick of a split tongue between two rows of teeth.

"Delina, my darling," he cried, his mind reaching to touch hers. He screamed when his thought tendril encountered an evil mind.

The gleam of a sharp blade, falling, stabbing.

He stood beside the altar, staring at the protruding hilt between her breasts, the swelling redness on her white skin.

Suddenly, she sat up, her mouth opened to reveal long sharp teeth. Then she laughed with a hollow, mocking sound.

Drawing up her legs, she let them fall open to reveal the black, hairy triangle between them. "Make love to me," she whispered with

51

a deep, hollow voice.

Her blue eyes glowed suddenly with a red fire. He looked with revulsion at the thin and forked tongue playing across her full lips. Against his will, he moved between her legs. She grasped his pulsating rod and guided him into the moist opening. As he pushed deep into her, he felt the searing pain as something with sharp teeth clamped tightly around his penis. With a cry, he pulled out, his hands reaching for the long, sinewy thing attached to his organ.

"Here," the girl said, handing him the knife she had pulled from her chest. He reached for it, chopped down hard, and watched the repulsive creature fall writhing to the ground.

As the snake slithered away, he saw the thick, fleshy thing it carried in its open maw. Looking down at himself, he stared with horror at the emptiness between his legs where a long rod should have been.

There was no blood. Looking at the girl, he noticed her swollen belly.

"I will bear you a son," she said and, throwing back her head, she laughed with a strange hissing sound.

Between her legs appeared the head of a snake.

"No!" he screamed, chopping down with the knife.

As the scaly head fell to the ground, it changed into the head of a human infant. He screamed silently. Sinking to the ground, his hands reached for the small head. They closed around nothing.

He lay on his back and looked into the face of Delina, who bent over him

"Hektor!" she called.

Her voice sounded so far away.

"Hektor, wake up!"

He woke to stare into a pair of dark worried eyes.

"Hektor," Azur said. "Wake up. We have trouble."

Chapter Seven

"Mongo-hunters," M'Tay said and spat into the water. Gone was the big smile and dreamy look from his eyes. He stood in the boat, a heavy bow in his hands, an arrow nocked, aimed at a group of men in a long, silvery craft floating on top of the water ahead.

Orion counted five individual, dressed in tight-fitting shimmering clothes. He saw the energy pistols strapped to their hips, but none of them had drawn a weapon. They didn't appear to be worried about the primitive weapon in M'Tay's hands.

Orion knew why.

An arrow would never penetrate the material of the suits. It would only leave an ugly bruise, painful but not lethal.

"We are friends," one of them called, showing his empty hands. "Can you understand me?"

"We understand," Azur said when M'Tay didn't answer.

The speaker from the other boat looked at Azur and grinned. Turning to the others, he said, "A girl, boys, and good looking too. I've heard these native women like to fuck, unlike the men. Apparently, the women are always horny."

The others laughed. "Maybe we can show her how real men do it, eh? What do you say, boys?"

"Sounds like fun. I haven't had a good lay for a long time." The man who had spoken was short and heavyset. His arms and legs bulged with thick muscles.

His companion laughed again. "Let us have her first, Storm. Once you put your huge lizard into her, she won't like us anymore. You'll split her in two, you big ape."

Storm grinned and flexed his muscles. "Try and stop me!" Leering at Azur, he called, "Prepare yourself, girl, you're about to gain an experience you'll never forget."

"You'd better not lay a hand on me, Mongo-stealer," Azur said coldly.

"Look at that." Storm grinned hugely. "She's got fire. That will add much to the pleasure." He looked at one of his friends. "Get this thing closer so I can step across."

As the silvery craft started moving, M'Tay spoke sharply. "Stop right there!"

The five men laughed. "Are you going to hurt us with that

toothpick, boy?" Storm taunted him. Suddenly, he held a blaster in his hand, but before he could level it, the twanging of a bowstring echoed loudly from the cavern walls and M'Tay's arrow knocked the weapon from the man's grasp.

Storm bellowed angrily and reached with his left hand for the gun of one of his companions.

Orion sat up, his own small energy gun in his hand. "You touch that weapon, my friend, and it may be the last thing you'll ever touch!" he said harshly.

Surprised, Storm stopped his movement and stared at Orion and at the gun. "I've never seen these natives use one of those guns before." Scrutinizing Orion closer, he said, "Who the hell are you? You don't look or sound like one of them."

"He is my husband," Azur said.

"Your husband?" Storm laughed and turned to his companions. "It seems to me we've run into a sympathizer, a native-lover."

While the others laughed and made lewd remarks, he stared again at Orion. "I'll forget what you said, lover-boy, and I'll give you a second chance. Now put that toy away and let me have the girl. I'm sure she won't mind."

Orion put a tight sizzling beam into the bow of the craft, melting the small figurine that had adorned it.

"Hey, the bastard ruined my mascot!" yelled Matt, drawing his gun.

Orion burned it in his hand. Cursing, Matt threw the weapon into the water, where it exploded moments after. At the same time, M'Tay put an arrow through the hand of one of the others, who had reached for his gun.

The boats were touching now, and two of the Mongo-hunters jumped across, one of them grappling with Drom, who had only been watching so far. The other man went for Azur.

She slapped him hard in the face and gave him a shove. He staggered back, lost his balance and toppled into the river.

Orion, who had been watching Storm, reached for Azur when she nearly followed her attacker into the water. Trying to steady her and the boat, which was rocking dangerously from the fighting of the two men in the bow of their boat, he was forced to take his eyes off the short, heavyset man.

When he looked up, he stared into the barrel of a gun.

"Enough of this foolishness!" Storm said cruelly. "Looks like you people need to be taught a lesson."

He fired his gun. The reek of burned organic tissue wafted into Orion's nostrils. He looked down to see a large hole in the bottom of the boat.

"Get ready to swim," Storm laughed, burning another hole into the dry material.

The water rushed in quickly now, filling the boat. Taking a chance, Orion threw himself across into the other boat. He could have entered Storm's mind, killed him, and taken over his body, but at the same time, he would have put himself into a vulnerable position.

His shoulder hit the other man's massive legs, throwing him off-balance. While Storm tried to steady himself, Orion grabbed for the gun, wrestled it away from the man. His head rang from the heavy blow Storm delivered with a big fist. Orion took hold of the muscular arm, twisted and heaved his opponent overboard.

His mind open now, his senses were tuned in to the dangers around him. An energy beam sizzled past him as he threw himself aside, then the gun in his own hand bucked slightly as he squeezed the trigger.

This time he had put his scruples aside after reading the killing impulses in the minds of their attackers. The beam from his gun sliced into the chest of the man nearest him, killing him instantly.

The remaining one stared at his dead companion and at the gun in Orion's hand, and then he threw himself into the river, swimming frantically toward the rocky shore.

Orion lowered his weapon. It served no purpose to kill the man.

The boat rocked as someone tried to climb back into it. Orion looked into Storm's cold and crazy eyes, read the killing fury in the man's mind. He waited until the heavyset Mongo-hunter was halfway in the craft, then he stepped closer and kicked him hard in the chest. Storm cried out hoarsely and fell back into the water.

"Take the other boat," Orion called to him, grinning. He turned to help Azur out of the water. M'Tay was already aboard. He looked around for Drom and found him floating a short distance away. Even in the semi-darkness of the cavern, he could make out the red stain spreading around him.

A fleeting mind touch confirmed his suspicion.

Drom was dead. Not far from him another body floated. At least he had not died alone.

M'Tay followed Orion's gaze and nodded grimly. "He died a

warrior, but I shall miss him." Then he spat into the water. "Before the offworlders came we had only the beasts to fight; now we must defend ourselves against men."

"You mean there was never war between the tribes?" Orion asked, perplexed.

"War?" M'Tay said. "For what reason? We may be of different tribes, but we are all..." he paused, searching for the right word. "...friends...no, not friends. We are all brothers. Why would I want to kill a brother?"

"Yes, why indeed?" Orion said with an ironic smile. "If you want to roam the stars you still have a lot to learn...brother."

* * * *

The new vessel was sleek and roomy, with a small cabin below deck. They would be traveling in comfort from now on. Orion studied the controls and turned the craft around.

"Go below," he told Azur. "Rest for a while."

She nodded and followed his request. M'Tay joined Orion at the controls and sank into the seat beside him. "Teach me how to use this and we can take turns," he suggested.

Orion smiled. "You are a very curious young man. I can see why you are so restless here among your people."

M'Tay watched him as he maneuvered the craft into the middle of the river. "Looks easy," he said.

"It is easy, once you have mastered a few basic facts." Orion smiled again. "Technology has its advantages now and then." He gestured at the cabin. "Comfort, of course, and this." He switched on the powerful headlights and increased the speed.

"Be careful," M'Tay warned. "There may be obstructions in the water."

"No problem. The computer takes care of things like that. Even with the controls on manual it will override and take evasive action automatically if anything pops up ahead of us."

The silvery craft glided silently across the water. In the bright glare of the headlamps, Orion could see the gaping holes in the walls on either side of the river. Entrances to caves or tunnels. Once, he saw a bulky shape moving back into the darkness, but not before he had noticed the glint of the chitinous body.

Another time something long and sinuous lifted a narrow, toothed head above the water surface, and then it disappeared again into the darkness of the water with barely leaving a ripple behind.

He watched M'Tay handle the controls for a while, satisfied with the youth's performance. "I'm going below," he told M'Tay, who nodded and proudly smiled.

"Don't worry about anything." The youth grinned. "I can handle this machine."

Orion closed the hatch and stood quietly for a moment. When his eyes adjusted to the semi-darkness inside the cabin, he saw the sleeping figure of Azur on the bed. The position of her body, partly on her side, partly on her stomach, exposed her shapely naked backside to his gaze. He could see the fleshy lips of her vagina below her buttocks. The sight caused a sudden pounding in his loins.

He stripped and lay down beside her. Gently, his hand caressed her buttocks. She sighed in her sleep and stirred but did not wake. His fingers traveled between her thighs, and then he began slowly massaging her soft pussy-lips.

His penis hardened and he moved into position behind her, the head of his swollen member gently touching the entrance to her love channel. He did not force himself into her, just moved the slippery glands back and forth between those satiny lips.

He became aware of a change in Azur's breathing, felt the stiffening of her body, and then she pushed her buttocks against him. His hard penis slid easily into her warm moist interior. He lay without moving behind her while the muscles of her vagina gripped his organ tightly and squeezed it with a gentle rhythm.

After a while, she moaned and began to move her pelvis slowly back and forth, increasing her tempo as she milked him forcefully. He grabbed her hips to steady her. Every time she pushed back, he plunged deep into her sucking sheath. She whimpered and clawed at the wall, her buttocks whipping against him.

Suddenly, she shuddered and lay still, only her inside muscles alive. His hand took hold of one of her breasts, his fingers dug deep into the soft flesh. She put her hand over his and squeezed tightly.

"Make love to me from the front," she moaned.

He pulled out and she turned around, spreading her legs wide. He moved between them and slid his penis back into her inviting love channel. She kissed him hungrily, straining against him. Again, she shuddered, her legs wrapped around his thighs.

He couldn't contain himself any longer and, with a deep moan, he let go and pumped his hot liquid into her. He crushed her against him, bruising her breasts as he did so. His mouth clamped over hers, cutting off the scream of ecstasy as she joined his tremendous climax.

Then he fell back. Exhausted and breathing hard, he lay beside her, his eyes closed. He sensed her above him and knew she studied him. He felt the slight tingling sensation as her long hair touched his chest.

"I love you," she whispered. She covered his body with hot kisses.

He smiled and drifted into a deep sleep, giving in to his body's demands.

He woke from a dreamless sleep. His hand groped for the girl but found her gone. As he became aware of his surroundings, he realized what had awakened him. On the floor beside him, Azur was on her elbows and knees, her posterior up high. Behind her, M'Tay knelt between her spread thighs, moving with a steady rhythm. Every time he pushed his stiff member deep into the girl, his lean belly hit her fleshy buttocks with a loud smack. Grunting with each thrust, he moved like a man in a trance. From the glazed look in his eyes, Orion knew the reason for it.

The Mongo.

He sensed the hypnotic impulses. Already he felt the desire taking hold of his own mind and body.

He watched them copulate for a long time, his eyes riveted to the spot where their bodies joined. M'Tay shuddered once in the throes of a climax, but he kept right on going.

Azur moaned and bucked beneath the young man, her fingernails scratching the smooth floor every time she experienced her orgasm. She had many but gave no indication that she had enough. M'Tay seemed to have come to his limits and pulled out. Exhausted, he sank to the floor.

Orion's own sexual urge became almost unbearable. The girl's buttocks still quivered and moved up and down. Moaning, she called for M'Tay to continue. Orion slid from the bed, moved behind her and his painfully swollen pole found her well-lubricated and waiting orifice.

Grunting, he buried his member to the root. Azur cried out loudly, but Orion knew he didn't cause her any pain. With mighty shoves, he took her and she met every one of his thrusts, sobbing loudly each time he pushed into her. He fucked her for a long time until he felt his own climax rushing to the point of no return. He lunged once more, his weight pushing Azur to the floor. She pressed her buttocks up against him, her inner muscles sucking on his gushing member until she had drained every last drop from him.

Then they lay unmoving, both of them breathing harshly.

She was the first one to move under him. "You are heavy," she breathed.

He rolled off her, and then he watched her peel off the transparent film of the Mongo from between her thighs.

As soon as she had it removed, Orion felt the dazed feeling leave his mind.

Azur gave him an apologetic look. He sensed her unease. "I hope you are not angry with me for what I did, but last night, when you finished making love to me, I still was not satisfied. When I saw the Mongos, I..."

Orion smiled and touched her hand. "It is all right, Azur. I have no right to tell you what you can or cannot do."

She kissed him. "I love you; you know that, don't you?"

"I know." He looked at M'Tay, who lay sleeping on the bed and, grinning, he commented, "He must be exhausted."

The girl slapped him on the shoulder. "Don't make jokes like that!" she pouted. "He is a very nice young man." Wistfully, she looked at M'Tay. "And good-looking too."

Chapter Eight

After using the small lavatory, they both went on deck to check out their location. Orion had already noticed that the vessel had stopped moving. The bright searchlight shone on a vast expanse of water. Orion looked back into the direction from where he estimated they had come and found the mouth of the river where it entered the underground lake.

Huge pillars descending from the high ceiling interrupted the vastness of the lake. It would be easy to get lost here. Orion hoped that M'Tay knew which way they had to travel. There wasn't much they could do until the young man woke from his exhausted sleep, so Orion busied himself with studying the vessel they had acquired.

It did not surprise him that it could travel across snow or sand as easily as it did on water. It might come in handy.

"Do you have any idea how we can get out of this maze?" he asked Azur.

She shook her head. "I've never been here before. This is as new to me as it is to you. My people live south where they can exist above ground, even in the winter. In the valley, where I grew up, there was a huge lake that never froze over. A number of hot water springs kept the water at a warm temperature all year round. The valley was quite fertile and covered with lush vegetation. Maybe some day I can take you there."

I'd be very interested to meet your people, Azur."

A loud splash in the water close to their vessel made her grab Orion's arm. "This place makes me feel uncomfortable. I hope M'Tay knows where he is taking us," she whispered.

"I'm sure, he knows," Orion said with a low voice, straining his eyes to see what had caused the splash.

The water was quiet. An eerie silence hung over the lake.

Another splash.

This time, Orion saw the flicker of movement at the edge of the searchlight's beam. A dark shadow moved just below the surface of the water, and then a crested flat head broke the surface, large eyes with slit pupils stared into the light.

"What is that?" Azur clung to Orion. "It is huge."

Orion chuckled. "I thought you might be able to tell me."

"I've never seen anything like it."

The giant head, still partly above the water, glided closer, heading away from the glare of the light. Suddenly, the head shot into the air on, what looked like, a long sinewy neck. As it lifted above the water, a pair of leathery wings unfolded just below the head and, beating them furiously, the creature opened its long, beak-like jaws to emit an ear piercing hissing sound.

Now Orion discovered that, what he had mistakenly thought to be the neck, was actually the body of the creature. He saw a pair of webbed feet at the end of it. The creature began running on the surface of the water, completing a circle around the vessel.

It was quite a spectacle, and Orion couldn't blame Azur for screaming when the fearsome creature ran up to the craft, wings flapping and beak wide open. Just before it collided with them, it veered sharply to the right, barely missing the bow.

"Do something!" Azur sobbed, her fingers digging into his arm.

"I left my gun below deck," Orion said, watching the creature turning around and getting ready for another run at them. "I think you're safe in the cabin," Orion told Azur.

They turned when they heard laughter behind them. M'Tay stood watching them, an amused look on his face. "I see you've met the *Glaa-hn*, the terror of the waterways."

Still laughing, he put his fingers into his mouth and whistled shrilly. The Glaa-hn stopped its run abruptly, shrieked, folded its wings, and sank below the water surface, where it sat, only the two enormous slit pupils glaring at the intruders.

The sudden silence was almost painful to Orion's ears. Somehow, he felt like a fool when he studied the young man who bent over with uncontrollable laughter. "I assume this fearsome looking creature is harmless?" he asked.

"Harmless?" sobbed M'Tay, wiping his eyes. "No, it is not exactly harmless, because many an unwary traveler has been scared to death by its seemingly fearless attacks."

"Then why are you laughing?" Azur planted herself in front of the youth.

"You should have seen the expression on your faces." M'Tay grinned, looking slyly at Orion. "I was somewhat pleased to see a brave star traveler display some emotion."

Orion smiled. "Glad, you're amused, M'Tay, but I'm only human." Almost human, he added silently.

Pouting, Azur stared at the eyes in the water, and then at M'Tay. "What about this Glaa-hn? Why this spectacle?"

M'Tay shrugged. "It has not natural weapons, like a poisonous stinger, long sharp teeth, or great strength. That wicked looking beak is as soft as your..." he grinned, "your...ah...lips. Since its main food supply consists of lichen and fungus, it has no need for sharp teeth or claws, so when threatened, it uses the only defense it has: Size, large wings, speed, and the ability to scream. It's all show...a bluff."

Orion nodded. "I've encountered many creatures like this one on many worlds."

"It certainly did a good job on me," Azur said, throwing angry looks at the crested head. "I don't like to be scared like that."

Orion put an arm around her shoulder. "Neither do I. Be happy it was just a bluff." He turned to M'Tay. "I suppose you have an idea what happens next?"

The youth nodded and pointed in the direction of a large obstruction sticking out of the water in the hazy distance. "We head that way."

Orion took over the controls of the vessel again and, as they began moving, they heard the shriek of the Glaa-hn behind them.

Laughing, they watched the creature perform its grotesque dance on the water.

"It does look sort of comical," Azur commented, "but I still wouldn't want to meet it when I'm alone. I am hungry. I'm going to see if I can find us something to eat."

"The Glaa-hn is not just a dumb creature," M'Tay said. "It is actually quite intelligent, nearly as intelligent as a human."

"It didn't act very intelligent." Orion chuckled.

"No, but that is in the Glaa-hn's nature."

Azur came back up, carrying three plastic food bags. Thankful, Orion accepted his and began wolfing down the steaming food. "How do you find your way around in this maze?" he asked M'Tay around a mouthful of stewed meat.

The youth shrugged. "I've been here a few times." He pointed at one of the pillars. "See those signs? We follow them."

Orion looked closer found the painted symbols and nodded. "I was beginning to wonder, because I am hopelessly lost. In fact, even with those signs I still don't know which way."

M'Tay gave him a wide grin. "That's because you don't know where we're headed and that is why I am here, starman. To guide you."

The rest of the journey was quite uneventful and monotonous. Because of the many obstructions in the water, they had to travel slowly. Occasionally they would watch another Glaa-hn go through its routine of trying to scare them away, and at one time, one of them almost knocked Azur overboard with one large leathery wing.

According to Orion's timepiece, it was late afternoon, when suddenly he heard human voices. From out of the darkness appeared four long boats, each occupying six men.

Natives.

They stopped when they saw the silvery craft. Orion noticed the hostility in their faces and his mind picked up the frosty feelings toward the intruder.

M'Tay waved to them, called out, talking rapidly in the native language.

Suddenly, they chattered excitedly and dipped their paddles into the water to bring their boats closer to the craft. One of them, a tall, heavyset man, climbed aboard and grasped M'Tay's arm.

"These are my friends." M'Tay indicated Orion and Azur.

The big native looked at Orion and smiled warmly. "If M'Tay calls you his friend you can call me friend. I am Koy."

Orion was not surprised to hear him speak in Universal. He shook the outstretched hand, the gesture of friendship on many worlds. "Hektor Orion," he introduced himself. "I am honored to call you friend."

Koy nodded toward Azur, smiled, but said nothing, and then he climbed back into his boat.

M'Tay took the controls and followed the four boats, as they moved away. "These are the Glaa-hn-Torks, which means something like *Guardians and Worshippers of the Glaa-hn.*"

Before long, they came to a large beach. A group of naked children came running when they saw the boats approaching. They were followed by some men and women, all of them naked.

Orion saw their apprehension as they stared at the long silvery craft, but they broke into happy laughter, followed by body-slapping, and dancing when Koy called to them.

It didn't take much guessing what he had told them.

Some of the children climbed aboard and began chasing each other around the large deck. Laughing and giggling, they jumped back into the water when Koy yelled at them, but he was grinning hugely as he did so. They waded ashore and followed the crowd. Orion found the air humid and quite hot.

"Why is it so warm here?" he asked.

"There is hot water coming out of the ground in many places," M'Tay explained. The Glaa-hn-Toks are very lucky to have found this place."

"Yes, we are," Koy agreed. "We have warmth, plenty of food, and many caves to sleep in, but we have not been lucky with the hunt for Mongos."

"There are many Mongos on our ship," Azur said.

"Yes," M'Tay said, throwing a sidelong glance at the girl, smiling. "There are many and they are yours."

Koy turned toward two girls who stood watching them and spoke a few words. They giggled and nodded.

Orion saw them speak to some other adult girls, and then the whole group of them headed for the craft.

"We will celebrate tomorrow." Koy smiled. "Thanks to you, my friends. And thanks to the Gods of Fertility. Of course, you will be our guests."

I was afraid of that. Orion wasn't quite sure if it was welcome news.

The village, if it could be called such, was similar to the one where he had taken part in his first celebration. A high cavern with openings in the ceiling let the light stream in from above. The walls were pockmarked with entrances to smaller caves and tunnels.

He saw one area where the women did their cooking in large copper kettles. Many of the women were busy preparing the meals for supper, and the aroma that wafted into Orion's nostrils made him swallow a few times in anticipation. "Smells like fish," he commented to Azur. I haven't eaten that for a while."

She laughed. "Is that all you think of? Food?"

He grinned. "I enjoy a good meal, but that's not all I'm interested in."

"I know." She smiled. "I've noticed you looking over all these naked women. You probably can't wait until tomorrow night."

He shrugged. "I don't mind looking, but you're plenty enough woman for me."

They had arrived in a corner where many quilted mats were laid out in a large circle.

"Sit down," Koy invited them. "We will eat."

Orion noticed more such places where the villagers sat in a circle around one of the many large kettles. The women were passing around small containers filled with steaming food.

He took one of these containers when it was offered and waited until the others started to eat. It smelled delicious, and when he tasted it, he was not disappointed. He stirred the thick liquid with a small bone one of the women gave him and saw pieces of white flaky meat, spongy cubes of fungus, long thin strips of some kind of vegetables, and a couple of small boiled eggs. He didn't care much for the beverage, a milky liquid that tasted like three days old mead, but after the second mug, he felt it go to his head.

M'Tay seemed to have a great time. He talked about their journey and how they captured the silvery vessel. Orion didn't understand a word, but from M'Tay's gestures, he knew that a great epic was in the making; much of it most likely fiction, like most such great works.

He heard his own name mentioned a few times and noticed a couple of the girls studying him with great interest. One of them, a petite longhaired female with large, shiny eyes, struck him as exceptionally beautiful.

She noticed his eyes on her and smiled, winking with one eye. Then she giggled and whispered something to the girl beside her, a short, somewhat plump female with short, curly hair. Her breasts rested on top of her up-drawn knees.

Enough meat there to make two women happy, Orion thought and winked back. He emptied his third mug and asked for another one. Suddenly, the prospect of taking part in another fertility celebration looked quite attractive.

* * * *

He didn't know how long he had slept. When a soft hand gently touched his arm, he became instantly alert. The cave he slept in lay in deep darkness, but he could clearly see the outline of a slim female against the dim light of the cave entrance.

Kneeling beside him, she put a finger against his lips, and then she took his hand and pulled, motioning with her other hand for him to follow her. Recognizing the petite longhaired girl who had flirted with him earlier in the evening, he wondered what she wanted from him.

She led him through a series of dimly lit tunnels. He heard the rushing sound of water. They seemed to follow that sound. Finally, they stepped into a small cavern. A waterfall came gushing out of the rocks, creating a large pond of swirling water below it.

The girl stepped into the water, smiled up at him and beckoned. Then she swam away, toward the falls. Orion hesitated, but then he quickly undressed and took after the girl. The water was pleasantly warm. He detected the slight odor of sulfur in the air.

The woman swam through the curtain of water, and when Orion followed her, he was surprised to find a large cave on the other side of the waterfall. Glowing lichen growing on the ceiling illuminated the cave with a soft light.

He looked for the girl and saw her climbing out of the water onto a small beach. Three other females stood already in the yellow sand. He recognized the short plump one, the one with the big breasts. The other two were tall and slim.

One of them possessed a pair of small breasts and her face struck Orion as somewhat coarse, but the other one was a real beauty, with extremely long and shapely legs.

All four giggled as they watched Orion swimming toward them.

Something seemed odd. The closer he came to shore, the more beautiful they appeared to him. They still looked the same, but suddenly all of them had perfect bodies and radiant lovely faces.

When he stepped out of the water, he sprouted an enormous erection and he was panting with frantic anticipation. A part of his mind knew the reason, but he didn't really care.

Right now he wanted nothing more than sink his weapon into one of those soft, waiting sheaths.

Chapter Nine

They didn't give him much of a chance to choose. All four of the adult females closed in on him, touching his body at various places. He found himself deeply kissing an eager mouth, while a warm hand closed around his straining penis.

They pushed him onto his back, one of the females straddled him, and hot moistness sheathed his shaft. Another pair replaced the warm lips on his mouth and then the weight on his lower body was gone for a short moment, but only for a moment, and then a hand grasped his swollen organ, guided it into another hot orifice. He felt the sweet up and down movements of the tight, but soft walls ripple over his stiff member.

From time to time, the lips he was kissing changed and so did the slippery sheath sliding on his shaft.

They were five animals in heat, possessed by an insatiable sexual urge. Only a small part of his mind watched with detachment and, somewhat amused, as he tried to still the hunger of his body.

Until now, the women had been in control, but then he decided it was time for him to take the reins. He lined them up in a row, on their knees, their lovely buttocks raised. Then he moved behind the first girl, the longhaired one and, slowly, so very slowly, he pushed his pole into her welcoming love-channel. She quivered beneath him as he lazily moved between her soft thighs.

She pushed up against him, moaning softly, and he grabbed her rounded hips, held her still. Increasing his tempo, he hammered into her until she screamed and bucked. When she quieted down again, he pulled out and moved over to the second girl, the tall one.

She cried out when he entered her and began bucking immediately. Putting his hands on her shoulders, he rode her until she sank to the ground, her thighs pressed together, the walls of her vagina rippling down the length of his shaft.

The plump one with the large breasts was the next one. He took hold of her breasts, rolled her swollen nipples between his fingers. Her buttocks were large, but firm and well rounded. She felt tight as he pushed past her fleshy lips and she almost made him lose control, but he didn't want to stop yet.

The one with the coarse face demanded most of him. He kneaded her small breasts and let his hands travel over her lovely, firm body.

She had nicely shaped buttocks, and he watched them quiver as she milked his swollen mast. Finally, she cried out, clawing the sand as she climaxed.

He moved back to the smaller woman. She lay on her back, smiling, her legs spread apart wide. He rolled on top of her and kissed her smiling lips. As he entered her, she pulled her legs up high and he brought her to a shattering orgasm.

The other three females were on their backs also and he took all three of them, one after the other.

He reserved his own climax for the small, longhaired one. He looked into her shiny, beautiful eyes as his hot liquid pumped into her. His mind reached out for hers, entered it, merged with it. She didn't know what was happening, but he knew she'd never forget this moment.

Her eyes were large, her lovely face contorted into a mask of pain as she writhed in ecstasy in his arms. She whispered something in her language. He didn't understand the words, but he knew what she said. Her thoughts were as clear to him as his were to her.

"God of Pleasure and Pain. I love you," she whispered.

He kissed her gently and held her close. Then he withdrew, first his mind and then his limp penis.

Her eyes were closed now and she lay breathing deeply. After a while, she opened her eyes, smiled, and said something, but this time he didn't understand her.

He smiled, shook his head, and, gently, touched her cheek. "You're beautiful," he said, "and it would be easy to fall in love with you."

When he looked at the other young adult females, who sat watching, he noticed an unhappy, bewildered look on their faces. The tall, beautiful one crawled on her knees toward him, touched his penis, and started stroking him. Oddly enough, it began to rise and thicken.

Then he realized what had happened. He had taken over control and neutralized the impulses of the Mongos between their legs, but he had only climaxed with one of them; the three other ones were still not fulfilled and the Mongos were still emanating their desire.

Letting part of his control slip again, he felt the powerful urge. Mounting the tall girl, he brought her to another orgasm and shuddered when his own climax rolled over him between her opening and closing long, shapely legs.

Then he did the same with the other two.

Afterwards, when he lay exhausted among their sprawled bodies, he wondered where and how he had found the strength to have four terrific orgasms in a row.

These Mongos were truly magnificent little creatures.

* * * *

Awakening from a deep, exhausted sleep, he looked at the woman in his arms. Her long, black hair covered his chest and he couldn't see her face, but he knew who she was.

Remembering the night, he smiled smugly. This was surely becoming a memorable journey.

Possessing a strong sex-drive, he had never been one for abstinence, but never before had he indulged this much.

The female began to stir. Her hand accidentally touched his penis. She turned, lifted her face up to him, and smiled sleepily. Then her fingers curled around his already erect shaft. She sat up and straddled him. Slowly, she rubbed his slippery glans between the swollen lips of her vagina, all the while smiling sweetly at him. Suddenly, her breath quickened and, with a loud moan, she pushed down, engulfing his stiff pole with her well-lubricated love-channel. Her hips began to gyrate slowly. He locked eyes with her and he merged his mind with hers.

"You are beautiful," he said in his thoughts and she smiled, understanding.

Her fingers dug into the muscles of his forearm, her face took on a painful expression. He held her rotating hips, guiding her gently. She seemed to have a natural talent for sex, doing the right things without any conscious thought.

While he looked into her lovely face and admired the smooth lines of her body, he suddenly realized that neither of them was under the influence of a Mongo. She must have removed hers during the night.

Her black shiny eyes never left his face, and when they both climaxed, she cried out, almost screamed. Then she collapsed on top of him, her small breasts pressing against his chest.

After a short rest, she began covering his chest with hot kisses. Her legs were still spread, his semi-hard penis still buried inside her.

"I'm afraid I have awakened a hunger in you that I might not be able to still, my sweet girl," he murmured into her ear, nestling his face in the mass of her soft black hair.

She smiled and kissed him on the lips. Again, her hips began to rotate slowly, and he felt himself responding. He was hard in a short time, but he just lay back and let her do what she wanted.

With deliberate slowness, she moved on top of him, her hips barely moving, only the slippery soft walls of her sheath pulsed hotly over his penis.

He relaxed, enjoying her gentle lovemaking.

Pressure. Release. Pressure. Release.

All the time her sweet mouth covered his neck, his face, his chest with moist kisses.

Suddenly, she began to whimper. He took her quivering buttocks into his hands, dug his fingers deeply into the soft flesh. He held her tightly against him as he climaxed inside her.

Again, he must have slept, because suddenly he realized he was alone. He stretched and, slowly, he sat up. Then he climbed to his feet and walked over to the water. With a happy sigh, he sank into the warm liquid and let it soothe his tired limbs.

I have weak knees. Couldn't do this every night.

He grinned and floated on the water, happy and content. He sensed the thoughts of people on the other side of the falls, but they were unmarked by hostility.

These people were simple, uncivilized, but they seemed happy. He was content to enjoy this peace for a short time. Most of his life was usually filled with danger and death.

When he heard voices, he swam across the small lake, through the veil of falling water and into the pool on the other side. A few natives were splashing in the water. He recognized one of the naked figures. Many times his hand had roamed over her lovely form.

Azur.

She hadn't seen him yet. He dove and swam under water toward her, his mind searching for her familiar thought pattern. She squealed when his hand ran up between her legs and kicked with her feet. When he rose up in front of him, she laughed and sprayed his face with water.

"Where are you coming from?" she asked. "I missed you last night." Playfully, she put her hand between his legs. "I was longing for this."

Orion grimaced. "I must have wandered off after the evening meal. Too much to drink, I think."

"Well, there is tonight," she said, a mischievous smile on her lips.

"One night of rest should have been enough for you." Then she screwed up her face. "Oh, I forgot. Tonight the village will celebrate the fertility rites. Do you think you're up to it? You look a bit tired."

"Hmm." Orion smiled sheepishly and floated on his back beside her. "Maybe you and I could sneak away and have our own little celebration."

"That would not be polite, Hektor. No, we'll have to take part."

They swam back to shore, past a group of splashing girls. One of them was *Brighteyes*, as Orion called her, the girl who had lured him into that wild orgy. She winked and blushed, and then she dove away, her cute round buttocks above the water's surface for a teasing moment.

"I see you've got one admirer already," Azur said beside him. "She's very pretty. Kind of shy. Maybe she's one of the virgins being initiated tonight?"

"Virgin?" spluttered Orion, swallowing some water. He made for shore, climbed onto the rocks, coughing violently.

Azur arrived at his side and padded his back. "Are you alright?" she asked, concerned.

"I'm fine," he coughed, grinning foolishly, when he saw Brighteyes smiling at him from the water. Beside her, he spied the plump one, her huge breasts floating above the water.

Both girls giggled. They swam past him, floating on their backs. He could see the dark triangles between their legs, as they slowly opened and closed them, clearly teasing him.

He shook his head and looked away. This was insane! Could he think of nothing else but sex? These girls did something to him. He recalled what one of the Mongo-hunters had said.

These native women like to fuck. They're always horny.

Maybe it was true. Azur certainly kept him busy at night.

Perhaps that was the reason why the native men had no sex-drive, except when stimulated by the Mongo. If the men were as horny as the women were, they'd do nothing but screw all day and night.

Mentally shrugging, Orion searched for his clothes. He found them in an untidy heap and put them on. Better cover up my masculinity, he thought dryly, before all the women go crazy. I couldn't handle the whole tribe.

"There you are," said a familiar voice behind him. He turned to see Koy walking toward him.

"I trust you slept well last night?" The big man smiled warmly.

"While the women are preparing for tonight's celebration, some of us men will go on a Glaa-hn-hunt. Would you like to accompany us?"

Orion looked at Azur, who nodded slightly.

"I'll probably be in the way here anyway," Orion said. "I'd be honored to come along."

"It will be an experience for you, starman. Hunting Glaa-hn is our way to say thanks to the gods for our existence. Maybe some day we can tell you the legends about our people and the race of the Glaa-hn. You see, they are not stupid creatures but very intelligent. They have chosen to exist as primitive beings, alone in the depth of the dark water, while we chose to live in the light and among others of our kind."

* * * *

The water rippled softly along the keel of the boats as the Glaa-hn-hunters dipped their paddles into the somewhat murky liquid. The party consisted of four boats, each carrying six men.

Orion knelt behind Koy, who sat on a bench in the prow of the boat.

These boats were different from the one they had used leaving the Ren-village. Narrow and long, with thick, spongy walls, they seemed fragile, but Koy laughed when Orion expressed doubts about the safety of the craft.

"It is made from the shell of a *Dangcreeper*. It splits open when ripe, and then the larvae of the *Voye-beetles* crawls inside and devours the soft pulp. The larvae hatches and leaves the empty, indigestible shell behind. We separate the two halves and make two boats out of them. Besides being light, they are almost impossible to tip over."

The boats glided speedily across the water. Glow-fungus grew on the ceiling and on the pillars supporting the roof of the giant cavern, and once Orion's eyes had adjusted to the twilight, he could see quite well.

It wasn't long before the four boats stopped. They had arrived in an area with many large rocks cropping out of the water. The ceiling was high above them.

A warrior in one of the other boats stood up. He was of short stature, and when he shrugged off the thin fur cape he wore, Orion suppressed a surprised groan. Long black hair spilled over smooth coppery shoulders, almost down to the round shapely buttocks.

A young woman.

She turned and Orion saw the white stripe of glowing paint

covering her small breasts, her stomach, and the front of her legs. Then he saw the shiny black eyes in her lovely face.

"Brighteyes," he whispered hoarsely.

Koy turned to Orion and smiled. "She has, doesn't she? In fact, that is quite a correct translation of her name."

"What is she doing here?" Orion asked, keeping his face neutral.

"She is the sacrifice."

"The sacrifice?" Orion repeated, appalled. "Are you telling me she will be sacrificed to the Glaa-hn?"

"That is correct, but you needn't worry. She will not be harmed if everything goes well."

"I don't believe I understand."

"Just wait and watch."

The girl and two of the warriors, one of them seemed quite old and fragile, the other one tall and muscular, climbed a large, flat rock, almost like a small island. In its center rose a tall, round structure toward the ceiling. The second warrior carried something colorful in his arms.

Orion watched as they led the female toward the tall structure. She moved like a sleepwalker, or like someone in a trance.

The tall warrior opened the bundle he carried and fastened it to the girl's shoulders. Then he covered her head with a grotesque mask.

The head of a Glaa-hn.

Two fragile wings sprouted from her back. They tied her to the structure, facing the water.

The tall warrior jumped back into the boat, while the older one stayed behind. Orion watched him move around on unsteady legs.

"Lorb is getting old." Koy sighed. "He is the only one not affected by the Mongo. When he decided to become a holy man, he had his testicles removed. Now it is time for him to choose a successor."

"What is his function at this ceremony?"

"He must make sure everything proceeds as planned, and at the right time he must cut off the *Great Gland* of the Glaa-hn. It is vital he is not influenced by the Mongo."

"That is important, yes?"

"Yes. Very important."

"I can block off the Mongo's influence," Orion said. "Tell me what I must do."

Koy hesitated, and then he nodded. "If you can do this, you may be of great help. You see, the Glaa-hn also depends on the Mongo for its continued existence. We use that dependence to lure it into our snare. The Mongo will put it into a trance and confuse its thoughts. It will not be aware of its surroundings. When Lorb gives you the sign, you will cut off the Glaa-hn's reproductive organ. This will paralyze the creature for a short time, rendering it helpless."

Orion didn't ask any more questions and jumped into the water to swim toward the small island.

Before the boats started moving away, Koy called after Orion. "Please, do not interfere unless Lorb tells you so. Whatever happens, let it be. The girl is drugged and quite happy with everything that is going to take place. Remember, she is the sacrifice to Lord Glaa-hn and honored to be the Chosen. In her vision, the Glaa-hn will be a handsome young man."

Orion had reached the island and climbed on top of the rock. The old man was just in the process of putting something between the woman's legs.

Orion felt the stirring of his penis and realized what the old man was doing. He shut out the hypnotizing impulses of the Mongo and joined Lorb behind a rock, so they could watch the girl and the water in front of her.

The old man began to chant softly. Suddenly, he let out a piercing cry and followed it with his low chant. After repeating this a few times, he stopped and listened intently.

The water was quiet, calm. No sound reached Orion's ears, except for the soft breathing of Brighteyes and the old man's subdued, but ragged gasping for air.

The pounding of his own heart seemed loud. Even though Koy had assured him that no harm would come to the female, he still didn't know what to expect. Crouching, he stared at the water for a long time, straining his ears for any sound.

The appearance of a slight ripple in the mirror surface of the water made him sit erect, but the old medicine man held up a hand in warning. Again, he emitted that piercing cry.

Then the water suddenly came alive as the snakelike creature broke its surface. With spread wings and open beak, it ran toward them and stopped short in front of the woman. It screamed, flapping its leathery wings and began climbing up onto the rock.

At first, Orion didn't know what to make of the white, glowing thing under the creature's belly, but then he suddenly knew.

It was a penis. Shaped like and nearly the same size of the penis of a well endowed man, it stood erect and seemed to pulse with a soft light. Before Orion realized it, the Glaa-hn reached the woman and, with one fluid movement, it shoved the rigid member deep into the girl's vagina. Lorb put a hand around Orion's arm. His bony but strong fingers dug into Orion's biceps. When Orion looked at him, the old man shook his head.

It seemed to Orion that Brighteyes had moaned loudly when the creature shoved its glowing member into her. He didn't believe it was out of pain. Not quite believing what he witnessed, he saw her belly working feverishly. Her buttocks moved back and forth, escalating as she milked the white rigid piece of hard flesh.

The glow of the Glaa-hn's penis seemed to increase and soon it was like a shining beacon, blinking off and on as it appeared and disappeared inside the woman's clasping sex-organ.

It seemed insane to watch the serpent-like creature and the adult female go at it like two passionate lovers, their bodies slamming into each other with blurring speed.

Suddenly, Brighteyes cried out and clamped down hard. Her whole body began to shake and her buttocks quivered in the throes of an orgasm. The Glaa-hn stopped its back and forth movement and stood rigid as it pumped its seed into the girl.

So entranced by this incredible happening, Orion almost missed his cue. He became aware when the old man shook his arm. Almost without thought, he took the knife from Lorb's hand and moved toward the pair by the structure.

The Glaa-hn stood like a statue in front of Brighteyes, its penis buried inside her. Already, she began to move her lower body slowly back and forth.

Orion looked down at the rigid penis, as it slid out of the girl's vagina and back inside again. Coming out of his stupor, he waited until the woman pulled back her buttocks for a new thrust. With a quick movement, he set the knife against the root of that strangely human-looking penis and pushed down hard.

The knife sliced easily into the rigid but soft flesh, and before he realized it, he had severed it from the Glaa-hn's body. He stared at the wound and was surprised to see only a trickle of blood.

It was red. The long body of the Glaa-hn fell to the ground, where it lay motionless.

Orion held the white piece of meat in his hand. He had

involuntarily caught it as it slipped out of the female's sex-organ. It still had a soft glow to it.

The old man was suddenly by his side and, gently, he took the reproductive organ and the knife from Orion's grasp. Then he removed the Mongo from between Brighteyes' legs.

Orion heard the clamor of excited voices. When he turned, he saw the four boats coming swiftly toward the island. The men swarmed up the rocks and congratulated Orion on a job well done. A couple of them untied Brighteyes and carried her into one of the boats.

Orion threw one last look at the unmoving body of the Glaa-hn.

"It isn't dead," Koy assured him. "The *Great Gland* will grow back and the Glaa-hn will be able to reproduce during the next cycle."

"It pleases me to hear that," Orion said.

Chapter Ten

Orion sat by the girl's side, watching her chest rise and fall, as she slept her head in his lap, her beautiful face lit up by a happy smile.

He felt disgusted but knew he had no reason to be. On his travels among the stars, he had seen many strange things. Stranger and more bizarre than what he experienced today. It was not his place to judge customs and behavior of other races. And yet...it bothered him that this lovely woman, who he had made love to only the night before, had consented to have sexual intercourse with a monstrous creature like the Glaa-hn, even if it was intelligent.

What possibly bothered him more was the fact that she had enjoyed it. Even with her being a consenting adult and this part of their customs, it didn't seem right.

A bright light ahead of the boats interrupted his brooding thoughts. Somehow, he knew trouble was on its way. His fear was confirmed when he saw the large silver craft speeding toward them. It stopped and hovered at a short distance away.

Orion recognized a stocky familiar figure.

"We meet again," Storm said, grinning hugely, an ugly look in his eyes.

Before Orion could say anything, he felt the punch of the paralyzing ray of a *Shock-rifle*. He sat rigid, unable to move. Helpless, he watched his companions freeze as the same weapon sprayed them.

The silver craft moved closer. A couple of burly men jumped into the boat.

"Take the girl," Storm commanded.

One of the men lifted her up and handed her to Storm, and then he and his companion grabbed Orion and dragged him onto the deck of the other vessel.

"Let's kill all these native bastards," said one of the men.

Orion recognized him also.

A short and skinny man with a booming voice interfered. "No, we don't want that kind of trouble."

Storm walked up to Orion with a triumphant grin. "I owe you this one," he said, and then he kicked Orion in the side.

Orion felt only a dull thud as Storm's heavy boot connected with his paralyzed body.

"I know you don't feel anything now," Storm said, "but you will soon enough. It's something to wait for. You won't know when it's going to hit you. Sort of a little surprise." He kicked him again. "This is for my buddy, Matt, who was murdered by you…and this one's for Blake."

After that, they carried him below deck and threw him onto a bunk.

Brighteyes, who had not been hit by the paralyzing ray, lay stretched out on a bunk on the opposite side. She seemed awake, but her eyes were glazed over.

Then he watched helplessly as Storm took advantage of the helpless female. She moaned and writhed beneath the heavyset man and put her slim arms around his broad back.

"She likes it, the little whore," Storm panted. "I told you guys these native bitches are always horny." He grinned at Orion. "How do you like watching, you bastard? Your days of screwing this little jewel are over. After this, she'll realize what she has missed all this time."

Orion looked at him coldly, unable to move his head; only with great difficulty could he shift his eyes. He reached out with his mind, but it was useless. The shock-rifles were diabolical weapons, quite effective against telepaths, because of their ability to disrupt the electrical currents of the brain.

Furious, he watched as another man climbed between the girl's spread thighs. Again, it seemed as if she enjoyed it, but Orion knew it was the influence of the drug that had not worn off yet.

After the man was finished with her, Storm made her kneel on the floor and mounted her from behind. Orion noticed, that Brighteyes suddenly began to struggle in the man's hold, tried to get away, but he held her in a tight grip. When he was done, he just let her drop to the floor, where she lay whimpering. Her eyes were closed and her hands clutched her belly.

I'll get you for this, Orion swore silently, letting the image of Storm burn into his mind.

They weren't taking any chances with him. After a couple of hours, just as he began to feel his fingers and toes again, they gave him another dose with the shocker. It didn't hurt, not now, but it would be painful once he came out of it completely.

He didn't know how much time had passed. After the second spray with the paralyzing beam, he drifted into sleep. When he awoke, he became aware of being carried. With the awareness also came the pain.

He assumed they had arrived at their destination. As he turned his head slowly and painfully to see where they were carrying him, a dozen miners suddenly started hammering inside his skull. Through a haze, he saw the bright ceiling and walls of a corridor. Soon they entered a large room.

"Here is another one for you," one of his carriers said. "Take good care of him. He is a mean one."

"Mean and heavy," grumbled the second one.

They dropped him unceremoniously onto the hard stone floor and left.

"Well, let me take a look at you," growled a deep voice.

Orion watched the tall, bulky figure getting up from a chair behind a large wooden desk. An ankle length cape covered the speaker's body. His face made him appear human, but Orion knew he wasn't.

His deep purple, almost black skin color and the pair of thick, curved horns sprouting from his temples, revealed his true nature. He had red eyes and a small beard sprouting from his wide chin.

A goat-man.

His smile almost looked friendly. "So you're bad?" he said with his deep, rumbling voice. "Well…we'll see."

With a speed belying his great bulk, he came toward Orion and pulled him up close to his face.

Orion felt the goat-man's hot breath. It smelled of tobacco and spices.

"I am Gror and I am the law around here. You think you are big? I am bigger and could squash you like an annoying insect." He held something in his hand, something round. With deft movements, he put it around Orion's neck.

When it clicked, Orion knew what it was. A collar. A shock-collar.

Gror stepped back and grinned. "If you behave it will be easy. You'll have a good time, but should you step out of line, then this…!"

Orion screamed involuntarily as the shock traveled through his body. He had barely been able to deal with the pain he was experiencing as his body regained its feelings.

This carried him over his threshold of pain.

He fell to the floor and lay twitching.

The terrible pain stopped abruptly. He felt almost good, except for the miners who were still busy hammering inside his head and the ants crawling all over the rest of his body. His side, where Storm had kicked him, seemed numb.

"That was just a sample," Gror said, his red eyes like glowing coals. "It can be worse."

* * * *

Her name was Sheel.

She was a few centimeters taller than Orion, who stood close to one hundred and ninety centimeters and tipped the scales at two hundred and forty pounds. He outweighed her by about twenty pounds, but he'd probably have a hard time trying to outwrestle her.

The loose black cape hid her body and he could only guess what she looked like underneath. However, the way she moved told him enough. Muscles and bones.

She didn't have horns like Gror. Black, coarse hair covered her head. It hung down in a thick braid behind her back. Her face couldn't be called beautiful and soft, but Orion found something exotic about it and, under different circumstances, he would have felt attracted to her. She certainly had a wide, sensuous mouth, and when she smiled, she displayed white, even teeth.

She was smiling now, but it didn't fool him. She's like a cat, ready to pounce on a mouse, he thought as he looked into her red eyes.

"From now on you are a slave," she said with a surprisingly soft voice. "Gror tells me you have a reputation of being mean. Believe me, I am meaner. Don't think because I am a female makes me soft. I have killed men bigger than you...barehanded."

She cracked a whip, the tip barely missing Orion's face. "I am kind of old-fashioned. I like to use this instead of the collar, because of the sound effect." Laughing throatily, she cracked the whip again. "Then again, it doesn't mean that I won't use the collar if I have to." With those words, she pressed a small button on the handle of the whip.

The shockwave washing through Orion was weak compared to the one Gror had given him. Nevertheless, it still hurt. He didn't fall down this time, just stood rigid, his fists clenched to his sides.

Sheel smiled wryly. "You have good control. That's good."

His head was still buzzing, his side hurt, and his legs felt like they were made from rubber. He wanted to curl up and go to sleep.

The big goat-woman walked over to a control panel in the wall and punched a button. Moments later, a tall, thin woman rushed into the room. She wore tight-fitting coveralls, which accentuated her thinness, and if she had any breasts, they couldn't be very large.

After bowing to Sheel, she turned to Orion and looked him over. Her eyes were strangely pale and her hair pure white, making her appear older than she probably was.

"Take him into the fitting room and get him some decent work clothes, Ceanna, and then bring him back here. Don't dawdle, you know that upsets me, and you don't want to make me upset."

Ceanna nodded and motioned to Orion to follow her.

"She doesn't talk," Sheel explained. "She understands everything, but don't expect to have a deep conversation with her. Or anything else. She's an expert in the martial arts."

He followed the thin woman down a long brightly lit corridor. She walked softly on thin-soled leather shoes, with the graceful movements of a ballet dancer.

She looked back at him and smiled. He realized that she actually looked quite attractive, especially when she smiled. He returned her smile, trying to take only shallow breaths. His side was beginning to hurt again. With every breath he took, flashes of searing pain stabbed into his already throbbing head.

They stopped in front of a metal door. She touched the control panel in the doorframe and the door slid open. Then she motioned him inside. They entered a small room, bare of any furnishings, except for a bench on one side and a wall of shelves on the other. The shelves were filled with bundles of clothing.

With a few gestures, she told him to strip. He took off his shirt and threw it onto the floor. Then he began to undo his belt, paused, and looked at the woman who was watching him.

"Everything?" he asked with a wry smile. "Completely naked?"

She nodded and chuckled, but never took her eyes off him. When he pushed down his pants, he saw the flicker of interest in her pale eyes and one of her eyebrows went up slightly. The tip of her tongue appeared briefly between her teeth, but then she averted her gaze and walked over to the shelves.

Pulling down a package, she handed it to Orion. He unwrapped it and took out a pair of pants and a shirt. When he put them on, they fit almost perfectly.

"You have a good eye for size," he said, smiling at his own pun.

She nodded, keeping her face neutral, and then she took him back down the corridor. Sheel waited for them, and after Ceanna left, the big woman attached a long, thin chain to his collar and, holding the other hand, she led him into another room.

"Just so you get used to the idea that you are now a slave." She smiled. "For all that it matters, you might as well think of yourself as belonging to me. I may be only a guard, but as far as you're concerned, I am your master. Your life and welfare lie in my hands." She yanked on the chain. "Understand?"

"Yes," he said, trying to hide the coldness in his eyes.

She laughed haughtily, her finger on the button that controlled his collar. "You know, I have a feeling there is more to you than you let on. I'll be watching you more closely. I might even decide to like you. Now, come with me!"

They stepped into an elevator, and her hand moved across the control panel. The elevator began to move down. When it stopped, the doors opened into another well-lighted empty room. He saw three doors, one in each of the visible walls.

"As you probably have guessed, we are underground. Not too deep, but deep enough. This is where you'll be spending your time from now on, unless…" She studied him, a calculating look in her red eyes. Then she shrugged. "Never mind. We'll see."

She thumbed the control to one of the doors. A narrow skimmer waited on the other side, beyond it stretched a dimly lit tunnel into the distance. As soon as they boarded the skimmer, it began to move and, gaining speed, it shot down the long tunnel. The glare from the bright headlights of the skimmer was reflected in the curved ceiling and walls of the tunnel. The skimmer came to a stop, and when Orion stepped through a narrow door in the tunnel wall, he knew it would not be easy to escape from this place.

However, that didn't mean he wouldn't try. *If they think I'm staying here for the rest of my life, they are out of their minds.* There was no question what this place was.

A mine. A Krill mine.

Chapter Eleven

It was hot.

Wiping the sweat from his brow, Orion returned to the backbreaking job of digging. The Krill-crystals were very delicate and shattered easily in their natural form. Only after undergoing a restructuring through a molecular processor, they became nearly indestructible and usable.

The crystals were found in pockets of a soft sand-like substance, packed hard from the pressure of the surrounding rock, which was cut away with lasers. The Krill-crystals had to be dug out with spades, carefully and gently.

Emptying his spade-full of dirt onto a moving conveyer belt, he straightened and looked at the little man digging beside him. "Hey, Cerlus," he called. "Any luck?"

Cerlus stopped and threw his spade to the ground. Spitting out a long string of curses, he reached for the water bottle hanging from his belt. "Nothing," he croaked hoarsely. "Not even a sliver for the last hour. The bitch is going to have our hide. She'll claim we're hiding it someplace."

He took a long swig from his bottle and wiped his mouth with a dirty forearm. "She's crazy, you know. Likes to inflict pain on people." He grinned. "I also hear she likes to fuck. She's horny as hell. A real bitch."

He cried out and ducked, lifting his hands to cover his face. A loud *crack* echoed from the tunnel walls, and an angry welt erupted from the little man's bare grime stained back.

"Watch your tongue, slave, unless you want it cut out of your loose mouth!" Sheel glared at Cerlus and cracked her whip again, but this time only for the sound effect.

Orion had known she was close, but hadn't realized how close. His mental guard was not always up, because so far he had found no need for it down here.

"I was only kidding, your Highness," groveled the little man, crouching on the ground. He couldn't hide the sarcasm and hatred from his voice. "It's the heat, you know. It scrambles my brain."

"Your brain has never been in any other condition," she said coolly. "Now, get back to work. You haven't produced anything worthwhile all day." Her gaze shifted to Orion, who stood, watching. "You too!" she shouted. Then she laid the tip of her whip across his naked shoulder.

It didn't bite deep, but it stung, and he felt the small rivulet of blood mix with the grime and sweat. His eyes narrowed the urge to tear the whip from her hand and using it on her, a strong desire, but he knew it would be a futile thing. He could overcome her, of that he felt confident. Much good it would do him; he'd never get out alive.

Controlling his anger, he resumed digging. His time would come. This wasn't it.

When the giantess stalked away to check on another group of slaves, the little man threw down his spade again. "I'd like to get my hands around her neck and squeeze until her red eyes pop from her head," he said under his breath.

Orion chuckled. "Why does she wear that black cape all the time?"

"Who knows." Cerlus shrugged. "Maybe she's so hideous underneath she wouldn't dare to expose herself."

"Anybody ever try to escape?" Orion asked, changing the subject.

"Oh, sure. The problem is getting topside. These damn collars send out a signal that is received by a computer. Our whereabouts are known at all times. No way to get by any controlled exits."

"How could a person get rid of the collar?"

Cerlus laughed. "You try to force it and it will blow your head right off your shoulders. Sheel keeps the coded release keys and I'll doubt if she'll oblige you by giving it to you." He shook his head and stared at Orion. "There is no way out of here, my friend, not even when you're dead. You'd better face it...we're here to stay."

Orion's face was grim. "I can't accept that, Cerlus. There must be a way out of here. I hear there are not only slaves working the mines, they also employ paid workers."

"They do." The little man nodded. "They're the ones who work with the lasers. Don't expect any help there. Those guys are worse than the guards. They'd have no qualms cutting down a slave, just for the fun of it. We're only meat. We don't exist. Most of the slaves down here are criminals, drifters, or guys who were kidnapped on other planets. Nobody knows we're here."

"I'll be missed."

"Missed...yes, but how will anyone find you?"

They worked on in silence. Shortly before their shift was over, Orion was lucky enough to find a large crystal. Very carefully, he dug it out and carried it to the area where other slaves separated the Krill-crystals from the dirt and sorted them according to size.

Ceana, who was supervising the pickers, most of them female, gave him a little smile when she saw him walking up to her.

"That's quite a nice specimen. It should make Sheel happy," said one of the women. "Maybe Ceana can persuade her to give you an extra ration of food."

"Wow!" Cerlus exclaimed behind Orion. "That would really be generous of Ceana."

"Don't be stupid, Cerlus," the woman chided him. "We all know you don't like Ceana, but she's never done you any harm."

"Not me, but she killed Romm."

"That was an accident. It was his fault, he tried to rape her."

"Pah," Cerlus spat. "How could he help himself, after she put that damn Mongo between her legs."

"He was caught trying to escape. Ceana had no control over the situation," the woman said hotly, glaring at him.

Ceana put a hand on the woman's arm and shook her head. Then she stared at Cerlus and pointed toward the exit. The little man let out a deep breath, turned sharply and stalked away.

Orion followed him slowly.

"She's strange, that pale-eyed bitch," Cerlus muttered when Orion caught up with him. "I don't think she's human. She's down here voluntarily, you know. She never takes time off, spends most of it down here."

"Is she a guard?"

"Not really. She is more or less Sheel's right hand. I don't trust her, and if I were you, I wouldn't either. Be careful. I saw the way she smiled at you."

"She did, didn't she?" Orion said carefully. Maybe there'd be a way after all. "By the way, what did that woman mean when she said Ceana killed your friend? And what about what you said?"

Cerlus shrugged. "Like she said, Romm tried to escape. I warned him, but he wouldn't listen. They caught him. But that's past history; I really don't want to talk about it." He gave Orion a sharp look. "You may get a chance to see that bitch in action. There's always some fool who thinks he can get away. Let's just hope that fool isn't you."

He fell silent as they joined another group of grimy and sweat stained slaves. One of the other men had a series of long, bloodstained cuts on his back. Another one leaned heavily on his partner as he dragged his left leg behind him. His pant leg was blood-soaked and ripped to shreds.

"Sheel's handiwork," Cerlus remarked grimly when he noticed Orion's interest. "She loves to play."

* * * *

Orion lay on his bunk, listening to the deep breathing sounds of Cerlus. One thing about the little man, he had no trouble sleeping. The other two slaves, who shared their sleeping quarters, were also fast asleep.

He wondered what had happened to Brighteyes. Somehow, he felt guilty about her fate. If it hadn't been for him, Storm might have left her alone. He thought of Azur, but didn't worry much about her. She was safe enough with the Glaa-hn-Tokks. No harm should come to her there.

Vaguely, he registered the presence of someone approaching in the corridor outside, but he didn't give it much thought. Only when a shadow appeared in the entrance, stopped and entered, did he become fully alert.

It was too dark in the room to see who it was, and he was reluctant to use a mind probe, since he received no danger signals.

A soft rustling told him that his visitor seemed to be getting undressed. He glimpsed a vague outline of a naked breast against the dimly lit frame of the brighter doorway, and then a warm nude body joined him under the covers. A pair of hot lips searched for his and his hand closed around a small but solid breast. The woman moved on top of him, her hand slid between them, found what she was searching.

Slowly stroking his already stiffening penis, she never removed her mouth from his. Almost brutally, she forced her tongue between his teeth, leaving him with the distinct feeling of being raped.

Guided by her hand, his engorged organ entered the slippery, hot wetness between her legs, and soon the mystery woman's passion swept him away. Letting his hands travel along the outlines of her slim body, the firmness of her flesh did not surprise him. He felt the rippling of strong muscles as she churned above him. She pulled up her knees, gripped his hips the way a rider would his steed and took his rigid pole into her as deeply as she could.

He held back as long as was humanly possibly, and when his

time came, he grabbed her buttocks and crushed her to him. He felt himself erupt inside her with tremendous force and just concentrated on the pleasure he experienced. Her mind touch came unexpected, took him by surprise. It was so strong, he could barely believe it.

Welcome, she said inside his head, bubbling with silent laughter. Her thoughts blended with his. He could have pushed her out, but her thoughts were open and honest as she surrendered herself to him. The ecstasy became nearly unbearable, their bodies writhed violently, and their minds caressed each other, became one for a long, glorious moment.

Then the ecstatic feeling gently subsided. Reluctantly and almost painfully, they drew apart. Although their bodies were still joined and their minds still touched, they were again two separate identities.

You have a strong mind and good control. I never guessed, he said. *How did you know what I was?*

Ceana chuckled inside his mind. *It's my special gift. I can recognize a telepath at first sight. Even your strong shield could not hide it from me.*

Why did you come to me?

Her powerful thighs clutched his hips. Inside his head, she giggled. *After what we just experienced, you still ask?*

Chuckling, he squeezed her firm buttocks. *I'm sure you should have no trouble finding a lover among the others.*

A lover, yes, but hardly anyone I could communicate with like with you, nor trust.

Trust?

Yes, trust. She kissed him. *Nobody must know what I am. Especially not Sheel.*

Why not?

She would have me killed, as she would you. She hates telepaths. You see, on the planet where she comes from, they believe in the superiority of the physical body. Deformed children are killed at birth or later, if they should develop certain unwanted traits.

I don't think I understand, Ceana. Telepathy has nothing to do with the physical body. Orion thought of his own body, strong and physically nearly perfect. He also believed in developing a body that was fit.

It shouldn't...not usually. A long time ago on her planet, people with extraordinary gifts banded together, formed separate groups. Telepathy was the most common gift. It became a religion. Some of the people believed that the mind was the greater thing, the body was not important. They developed their minds, but neglected their bodies. Grotesque beings were born. They almost became the norm.

Why would they not look after their bodies? Orion asked. *After all, a sick body cannot house a healthy mind, not for long.*

That is true. There were still many people with no mental abilities, so they perfected their bodies. Finally, a terrible war broke out. It lasted for decades, until the so-called normal people with their superior physical strength wiped out most of the freaks.

Sounds very familiar, Orion said. *Throughout history, people who were different have been persecuted on most planets. The color of their skin, their hair, the shape of their ears or eyes, their beliefs...you name it and someone will find a reason to call you different, a freak, and hate you.*

I know, but I don't consider myself a freak. Ceana snuggled up to him and pressed her warm body against his. *Do you? Do you think we're so different from most people? We eat, sleep, breathe. We hate, we love.* She kissed him gently. *We need to be loved. I need to be loved.*

Holding her close, he sensed her loneliness, the terrible hunger inside her. They were strangers, and yet...their lovemaking, the joining of their bodies and minds had brought them closer together than most lovers could ever hope to be. They had shared as much together as each was willing to give. Neither one had revealed their true feeling nor their innermost thoughts.

Orion could not allow anyone to know his true identity. No telepath, no matter how strong, could break through his deepest mental barrier. The alien awesome power was locked deep inside him and surfaced only when there was a real need.

Only a Carrier of the Ancient Memory, like himself, was able to understand the high-level impulses.

He understood her loneliness. He knew he was different and sometimes he longed for someone of his own kind. The remembered Lu-onna. For a short time, they had been together. They had not been lovers, but they had loved each other as only a man and a woman of their kind could love. Their joining had been complete with no holdback, no secrets. For a fleeting moment, they had known happiness.

Ceana's thoughts brought him back to the present. *You haven't answered my question, lover. You must have been far away. Thinking about a woman?*

Sorry, he said, stroking her gently. *No, I don't think we are so different.* He knew she needed to hear that. It seemed strange for a telepath to ask: What are you thinking? Nevertheless, they respected each other's privacy. Neither one was snooping around in the other's mind.

I am glad you accepted my gift to you. I was a little afraid you might reject me.

He chuckled. *A woman like you? Do you think I'm an idiot?*

She laughed. *There is something else.* Her thought impulses carried an undercurrent of unease. *Tomorrow I have to do something I do not enjoy, but I must do it to ensure my continued existence. I have no choice. Please, don't think wrongly of me.*

What is this thing you must do?

You'll see. Also, remember what I told you. Don't let anyone know what you are. She kissed him again and slipped from his embrace.

He watched her shadow as she hurriedly dressed and stared after her as she left the room on silent feet.

Chapter Twelve

"What's happening?" Orion asked as he slid into the seat beside Cerlus.

Other slaves joined them on the long, narrow platform. When all the seats were taken, the skimmer moved into the tunnel and sped up. Not far behind them, another skimmer followed, also loaded with slaves.

"This is one of the few times we get closer to the surface," the little man answered. His voice sounded grim.

"What's the occasion?"

"Somebody tried to escape. Of course, they caught him. You're in for a special treat, my friend. Something to remove all thoughts about any escape plans you might be hatching." He didn't say anything after that, nor did any of the other slaves.

The floating platform came to a halt and everybody got off. They were in a large cavern. From the high ceiling hung bright lights to illuminate the skimmers already parked and the ones coming through giant doors set into the walls. In the center of the cavern, a number of elevators provided the only way to get to other levels.

Guards, some human, some not, with weapons in their hands or claws, herded the slaves into the elevators. The doors closed and up they went. It didn't take long before the doors opened again to let the silent slaves enter another large cavern. From here, they walked in groups of ten, with two armed guards to each group, down a corridor that led into a huge circular cavern.

Tiers of seats ringed a large empty space in the center.

Orion had seen places like this.

This was an arena, divided into two distinct parts. One-half was already occupied, the other half quickly filled with the incoming slaves.

Orion looked at the people in the other half of the arena. One glance told him those were not slaves. Men and women, some of them dressed in gaudy clothes, some in some kind of uniform. By chance, he recognized one of the faces and his face muscles tightened momentarily.

Storm. The man responsible for his being in this predicament.

The stocky man sat beside a tall, gaily painted woman, who

appeared amused by something he said to her. As she pointed to a group of slaves, they both laughed.

Orion could have killed the man with one thought impulse, but it would have solved nothing. He didn't know how sophisticated a detection system these people had. He remembered Ceana's warning and he kept his thought shield closed.

He needed the man to find Brighteyes.

A loud amplified voice interrupted his thoughts.

"Honored guests, welcome. GESCOM has put together a great entertainment for you, and we have a special treat today. As you know, the government has sent us a few of its hardened criminals so they can pay back some of the wrong they have done to our peace loving society by working in the mines. They are treated fairly, not like criminals but as ordinary workers.

"Most of them are thankful for this humanitarian act and, after a short time with us, become law-abiding citizens. Unfortunately, not all see the error of their ways. They try to escape our lawful custody and therefore must be punished."

The voice paused. Orion looked at Cerlus, who was mimicking the speaker, "…and therefore must be punished." The little man spat. "If their punishment would only fit the crime. Watch how the Almighty GESCOM doles out just punishment, my big friend. Just watch and be thankful it's not you down there."

The amplified voice droned on, "Here is the first performance for your entertainment."

Two men, naked, their muscular bodies glistening with oil, entered the arena. They began circling each other and then they clashed together with a loud meaty thud. Both of the men were of equal size and agility. Matched even in strength, they put on a beautiful display, but it didn't arouse much enthusiasm.

After that, four women appeared, also naked. First, they went through a series of erotic dance movements and then they began to wrestle. Under different circumstances, Orion might have enjoyed it. Marvelously built, they moved with an ease and grace that showed talent and promised physical pleasure for any man lucky enough to gain their favors. It looked more like dancing, though, than a test of strength. They finished with two of them on their backs and the other two lying between their spread legs.

The visitors applauded lamely. One man yelled, "Get some men between their thighs and it will be much more interesting!"

Some laughed and some whistled loudly.

"Be patient, honored guests." The amplified voice chuckled. "Perhaps this will be more to your taste," The amplified voice said.

A group of naked little men came running through the entrance. The first thing Orion noticed was the large size of their feet and the huge, thick penis each of them had hanging between his short legs. It seemed way out of proportion to the rest of the body.

Between them, they dragged a giant woman. She looked fat and ugly, her gross body covered with scraps of tattered clothing.

The little men swarmed around her and tried to pull her down to the ground. Ripping the rest of her clothing from her hairy body, she was soon completely naked. Her swollen, huge breasts bobbed up and down as she tried to stay on her feet.

She roared like an enraged animal and kicked at the chattering little men. Orion did a quick count and counted eleven of them. Two of them lay on the ground, unconscious from a blow to the head, but the others didn't give up, and it didn't take long before they succeeded in their task.

One of them stunned her with a club he had produced from somewhere. She was out long enough for the little men to drive stakes into the ground, and then they tied her thick arms and legs to the stakes with pieces of strong rope.

By this time, all of the dwarfs sprouted enormous erections. The first one climbed between the giantess's meaty thighs and shoved his huge organ into her hairy cleft. Two others began sucking on her long nipples.

They took turns raping her. Every time, one of them climaxed, he let out a loud howl, while the others danced around the thrashing bodies.

The visitors clapped and laughed, but the disgusting spectacle didn't amuse Orion or the other slaves. Neither did the other slaves.

"Next a demonstration of the humane way we treat prisoners who decide to be rebellious. A collar around the neck sends electric shockwaves through their nervous system, rendering them helpless. Very effective and hardly painful." The voice from the speaker chuckled again. "Some might even enjoy it, as you will see."

"The bloody liar!" Cerlus cursed, rubbing his neck.

The giantess had been dragged away. The little men were gone. In their place stood a tall, robed figure.

Gror, the goat-man.

His curled, polished horns glistened in the overhead lights as he strutted around the arena.

Three ragged-looking individuals in slave's clothes stood a distance away from him, looking placidly at the giant guard. All three carried clubs in their hands, while Gror, apparently, appeared unarmed.

At a command from somewhere, the slaves began circling the goat-man. They rushed him at the same time, but none of them reached him. He let them come within a few paces, and then his hands moved together.

The slaves froze, their faces grotesque masks. Then they fell to the ground, bodies rigid, mouths open, but no sound escaped.

Gror lifted his arms and the three slaves stirred, staggered to their feet. The goat-man moved away from them, stood waiting.

Again, they attacked him. Again, they ended up on the ground.

"You see, ladies and gentlemen, didn't I tell you? They enjoy this. Why else would they keep attacking? Nobody tells them to do so."

"Why indeed?" Cerlus said beside Orion.

"Why don't they give up?" Orion asked the little man.

Cerlus laughed grimly. "Because they were promised freedom if they managed to touch the goat-man. They won't make it. Nobody ever does, but they'll keep trying."

So they did. Repeatedly, until they couldn't stand anymore on their feet.

"And now you'll witness the punishment of a criminal who thought he could escape." The commentator laughed. "Maybe this will change his mind."

Another tall figure, robed in black, strode into the arena, carrying a whip. Sheel.

* * * *

Sheel used her whip as skillfully as she had displayed many times. With cold-blooded determination, she laid the lash across the naked back of the poor prisoner who stood submissively in front of her and transformed it into a bloody mass. When he was carried out, another slave came out of the entrance. He charged Sheel the moment he entered the arena, but he didn't get very far. The whip cracked and the prisoner staggered, the leash wrapped around his neck.

She pulled hard. His hands went to his neck, his fingers clawing frantically, but she gave him no chance. He fell; Sheel moved in and pulled him up by his neck. Then she threw him across the hard ground. Moaning, the man tried to crawl away on all fours. She let him crawl a short distance, and then, methodically, as he crawled around to find an escape, she stripped the skin from his back.

He collapsed, unconscious, his blood staining the ground.

"The bitch!" Cerlus curse. "She enjoys every moment of it."

Sheel strutted around in the arena, cracking her whip. Then she took a deep bow and strode out.

The voice of the commentator broke into the cheering of the visitors. "The next demonstration is especially for you people from off-planet. You probably have heard stories about the Mongo, the little creature the indigenous people use in their fertility rites. We need six volunteers for this demonstration. The rest of you may place bets. How many will be able to resist the alluring emanations of the Mongo?"

Chuckling, the voice added, "And let's not forget the beauty of these females."

Six young women walked into the arena. Smiling and moving their perfectly formed nude bodies seductively, they displayed themselves without shame. They were painted like the native women Orion had seen, but he doubted if any of them were native to this planet.

He could sense the emanations of the Mongo between their legs, but the women were not close enough to have an effect on the watchers.

Six naked volunteers stormed into the arena, laughing and hooting. It was obvious that none of them had any intentions of resisting the irresistible call. Within thirty seconds, each of them had grabbed a woman and lay between her spread thighs.

"They're whores," Cerlus said, disgustedly. "Even without the Mongo they would have spread their legs." He spat, and then he looked slyly at Orion. "You know, I wouldn't mind being one of those volunteers right now. How about you?"

Orion grunted. "In a private place I guess I wouldn't mind. Those women are all good looking and seem to know their business."

He was watching a short, fat man, who was lying on his back. One of the women had straddled and impaled herself on his straining member. While she bounced on top of him, his pudgy hands kneaded her swinging large breasts.

Then his gaze wandered to another pair. When he saw the petite and dark-haired woman, he thought for an insane moment it was Brighteyes, but then he saw her large breasts and relaxed.

The man, a big, hairy brute, grabbed her from behind, lifted her up, and shoved her on top of his huge penis. Slowly, they sank to the ground, until she knelt in front of him. His large torso cupped her small, fragile looking body and his buttocks quivered as he rammed himself into her from behind.

Her own appetite seemed to match his. Her small buttocks pushed back against him with every thrust of his hips and her hands clawed at the ground.

All of the other couples were now locked together in various positions. Over the speakers, the grunts and moans of the participants of this orgy testified to the pleasure they experienced. Orion could see more volunteers lining up by the entrance to the arena. When the first six didn't seem to want to quit, the others called for more women.

They didn't have to wait long. Another batch of women spilled into the arena. Orion noticed a few older ones among them. Soon the other volunteers were pumping between the newcomer's welcoming thighs. Some of the others were changing partners. Two of the men shared one woman. One of the men lay on his back, his penis in the woman's mouth who was straddling him, her buttocks pushed high to let the other man enter her vagina from behind.

"Those bastards!" Cerlus let out a loud curse. "Those are slaves down there now. Some of them will probably get pregnant, because they are not on *preventers*."

"How do you know they're slaves?" Orion asked. "I see no collars."

"No need for collars. The Mongos control them." The little man scratched his crotch. "It's been some time since I sank my pole into a woman's pleasure maker while she had a Mongo between her legs."

"Honored guests," the voice came over the speakers. "It seems the party got out of hand. There's no telling when they will stop. Bear with us while we clear the arena."

A group of women, dressed in gray uniforms, came running into the arena. They threw large nets over the couples and dragged them out. When the arena was empty, another figure entered; tall, lean and naked, except for a tight-fitting skullcap.

Chapter Thirteen

She looked marvelous as she moved lithely about. Naked, her body not as thin, and her breasts much fuller than Orion remembered.

"Honored guests, may we present Ceana. We have developed a device that will enable her to neutralize the effects of the Mongo on herself. A prisoner, who has unsuccessfully tried to rape a female guard, will get his chance now with Ceana. He has been promised freedom if he manages to penetrate her." The voice chuckled dryly. "If he succeeds he will enjoy a good fuck and gain his freedom. Place your bets now. Will he be successful?"

Ceana stood in the center of the arena, her breasts and buttocks thrust out.

The prisoner was a big man, with long hair and a heavy beard. He looked at the naked woman, but made no move toward her. Orion noticed that Ceana held something in her hands. When she put them between her legs, he knew what it was.

A Mongo.

The prisoner's attitude changed abruptly. He grunted and charged toward the woman, like a bull in heat. Below his belly, his penis had become rigid.

Ceana let him come close, and then she twisted her body slightly, grabbed his arm, and flipped him onto his back.

Orion knew the man stood no chance against her, unless he was a martial arts expert, which Orion doubted. In addition, he would not be able to fight the impulses of the Mongo.

Ceana lay down on the ground, her legs widespread. As he threw himself between her long, open legs, she closed her knees. He hit them with a loud grunt, and then he sailed threw the air as Ceana pushed up her legs. When he came at her again, she bent down, knelt, her buttocks toward him. With a triumphant shout, he grabbed her hips, his stiff penis thrusting forward to enter her inviting sex-organ. Before he could slide in, she dropped to the floor, her legs shot backward, between his legs, and he sailed across her back.

The crowd roared.

After sluggishly getting to his feet, the big man approached her again, determined to mount her and win his freedom. She played with him, grabbed his stiff penis, pulled him toward her, and let the tip of his straining member touch the fleshy lips of her vagina. Mad with lust, the man pushed his body forward, but her buttocks pulled back. When he reached around her to take her buttocks into his large hands, she brought up her knee and hit him hard in the stomach.

His hands didn't let go. He pulled her to him, his rigid organ searching for a place to enter her body. Her head moved forward, smashed into his face. Then she laid the edge of her hand across his windpipe and rammed stiffened fingers into his midriff.

He collapsed and was carried away.

Ceana stood spread-legged, her hands high above her head.

When the crowd finished clapping and cheering, the commentator's amplified voice rose again over the clamor of voices. "As you have witnessed, Ceana is a master in the martial arts. A challenge: Any of you men out there think you can beat her? It will be rewarding."

A young man rose among the spectators and called, "I'll take the challenge. What is the reward?"

"Ceana is the reward. Just to make it fair, she will remove the Mongo.

The young man disappeared through an exit, and a few moments later, he joined Ceana in the arena. He was well built, his muscles smooth, not very defined, but they looked solid. Except for a leather jock, he was naked.

They bowed to each other and dropped into a fighting stance.

After a few encounters it became obvious to Orion that Ceana was by far the superior fighter. The young man was good, very skillful and he moved with ease and confidence, but he lacked Ceana's speed.

It was also obvious that she would let him win.

Suddenly, he had her pinned to the floor, on her back, her legs widespread. He ripped off the jock and plunged his stiff penis into her yielding vagina.

His amplified grunts and Ceana's heavy breathing was soon drowned out by the hooting and whistling of the spectators. He moved like a piston between her opening and closing thighs and, with a triumphant shout, he climaxed inside her. When he rose to his feet, he lifted his hand and, grinning, he strutted around like a gladiator after defeating a ferocious lion.

Beside him, Ceana stood expressionless. She was facing Orion and it seemed she was looking straight into his eyes. He remembered her words from the night before and he understood.

The commentator spoke again. "Until now, the fun was only for you male visitors, but to be fair, we have something to keep you ladies entertained. You may select one of the prisoners and he is yours for the rest of the day to do with as you please. Use your imagination."

While Orion was watching the flogging of another prisoner, somebody touched his arm. He looked up to see one of the guards.

"You!" the guard said harshly, "Come with me."

* * * *

"I'll be outside," the guard warned with a menacing look. "In addition, this place is electronically monitored."

Orion entered the room. It was luxuriously furnished with thick rugs on the floor. His eyes fell on the person sitting on a low divan. A woman by the looks of the satiny luminous robe that clung to her body. Her face was covered with a veil, only her eyes were visible. Dark, warm eyes, with crinkles in the corners, indicating that she was smiling.

"Come in. Don't be shy." Her voice sounded husky, pleasant. She got up and walked toward him. In her gloved hand, she held a crystal goblet. "Here, drink this."

She laughed throatily when he seemed to hesitate. "It is not poison. Just a little drug to make you feel relaxed and to give you stamina."

Still hesitating, he took the offered drink and emptied the goblet. The liquid had no taste. It might have been clear water.

"I'm sorry to rush you, but you're not here for conversation. Please, take off your clothing." She stepped back and watched him undress. Her eyes widened slightly when he was naked. "My," she said, a slight tremor in her voice. "You are a handsome specimen of a man."

He began to feel the effects of the drug. The room seemed to swim for a moment and he staggered, but then it passed and everything was back to normal.

He knew it wasn't.

"Aren't you getting undressed?" he asked, his voice heavy and thick.

She laughed again. "In good time, my dear. Now I just want to watch. There is somebody I want you to meet." She snapped her fingers and Orion sensed someone entering the room through a curtain-covered doorway.

He turned and looked. Then he gasped as he watched the lovely creature walking toward him.

The lines of her nude perfect body seemed to loose their sharpness for a moment. He blinked to clear his mind from the drug. Fleetingly he wondered why he had been given a drug. The young woman he faced was so beautiful, he didn't need any encouragement.

Her breasts were high on her ribcage, round with red long nipples. They bounced slightly as she seductively moved her body, her sleek muscles rippling under smooth creamy skin. She smiled, wriggling her hips enticingly. Then she fell to her knees, turned and presented her lovely buttocks. Between her slightly spread thighs, he saw the fleshy lips of her vagina, ready and waiting.

He licked his lips and dropped to the floor. As he knelt behind her, he felt hands touching his body, warm smooth hands that stroked his back, his chest. A naked body pressed against his back.

The other woman. He had been so enthralled with the vision in front of him, he had completely forgotten about the veiled woman. Her hands moved around his belly, found his erect penis.

"Push it into her...now...!" her voice whispered into his ear.

Guiding him, her hands fed his stiff organ into the waiting sheath. The woman behind him pushed him with her own hot body, forcing his penis into the wet orifice.

At first, it was tight, but then the buttocks in his groin moved, the thighs opened wider, pushed back against him, and he entered heavenly bliss.

"Take her slowly," the woman at his back whispered. "She likes that."

He moved slowly in and out of the satiny wet sheath. Behind him, the other woman had her thighs clamped around his hips. He felt her thick pubic hair tickling his buttocks. Her arms held him tightly and her hot breath caressed his neck. She moved with him, as he pushed deeply into the young woman's sucking love-channel.

She was incredibly tight. Without the inhibitor in the drug, he probable could not have lasted long. He pumped with steady movements. When he started to increase his tempo, the other woman slowed him down, gently but forcefully.

"Take it easy, lover. Take it slow. There is no hurry," she breathed beside his ear. Her hands grasped his scrotum, her long nails dug in gently, creating a slight sensation of pain. It only enhanced his pleasure.

When he finally climaxed, he heard a low growl. He didn't know where it came from and he didn't care. All that mattered was the pleasure he experienced.

After a sudden blur of motion, he found himself lying on top of a female body, cradled by two soft thighs, pumping rapidly.

Her arms held him close as she pressed her upper body against his. He felt her soft breasts against his chest, warm and pliable. Two passionate lips clamped over his and kissed him hungrily. There was a different feel to the hot walls rippling along his rigid shaft and he knew he was fucking the other woman now. Her vagina was not as tight as the one of the young woman, but she moved her lower body forcefully against him and her thighs were like a vice around his hips. Her heels dug into his buttocks and her fingers raked his back as she approached her orgasm.

"Now…now!" she moaned. "Climax now! I want to feel your hot sperm shooting into me. Come…come…come now!"

He obliged her wishes, came with a roar, felt his hot discharge erupting inside her clutching sheath. She pushed up, held him in a tight grip.

Something wet touched his back. The woman underneath him relaxed and released her hold. Putting her lips against his ear, she said, "Par wants you again. I'm sure you can oblige her."

He didn't remember pulling out of her. Again, he experienced that strange blurring sensation, and then he found himself kneeling behind the young woman. He felt her quiver as his stiff penis penetrated her, and slowly he pushed in and out of her tight channel.

"Take as long as you want," a voice whispered into his ear. "She likes it and so do I. Let me watch you two young lovers. I know you like to fuck her, because she is so wonderfully small and tight. Don't worry about hurting her. She can take it."

She moved away, but he knew she was close and watching. He didn't care. There was so much beauty here and so much pleasure. He must not climax yet, must prolong the pleasure as long as was possible.

He moved like a man in a dream.

In and out. In and out.

Into the smooth tightness…deep…deep.

Slowly back out. Then in again.

Finally, the moment came. It gushed out of him into her clutching sheath. Again, he heard the low growl fill the air; it rose to a keening wail.

It was over much too soon. Exhausted, he collapsed on top of the form under him.

* * * *

His head was suddenly clear and he looked around. He lay on a deep-piled rug.

A low chuckle made him turn his head.

"Well, the great stud has finally regained his senses." The woman who spoke lay supine on the low divan. Beside her, on the floor, sprawled a large feline. The yellow eyes seemed to study him intensely.

The woman was dressed again, the veil covering the lower half of her face.

Orion sat up and searched the room.

"Looking for someone in particular?" the woman asked.

"I'm not quite sure," Orion said, hesitating. "I seem to remember a young woman."

"You do, do you?" Her laughter was throaty and full of merriment. "There was no young woman."

"Oh, come on now." Orion was not amused. "I agree, I was drugged, but there definitely was a young woman. I remember her quite clearly."

"You are wrong. There was only me and Par." She laid a hand on the feline's head.

The great cat gave a low growl, never taking her eyes off Orion.

"Par?" he echoed. Getting to his feet, he pointed a finger at the cat. "Then who did I…?" He shook his head. "Are you saying I fucked an animal?"

"Not an animal," the woman said softly. "Par is an intelligent creature." Suddenly, her voice sounded scornful. "What makes you think only humans possess a superior intellect?"

He lifted his hands. "I apologize. I should know better. But still…she is so different. I…find it appalling. You have to admit, she looks like an animal."

"Does the outside form really make such a difference?" the woman asked.

"It shouldn't, but it does. Well, at least you are human."

Her eyes seemed to study him, and then her hand moved to her face and slowly she removed the veil.

Orion suppressed a shudder when he saw her face.

101

Only her eyes were human.

What he remembered to be a pair of soft lips was in fact only a round hole surrounded by a mass of soft tendrils.

He didn't see a nose.

"Horrified?" she asked. She opened her robe, pulled it off, and displayed her nude body. It was human-like, but definitely not human. When she pulled off her gloves, he discovered tendrils instead of fingers.

Her arms and legs were human in appearance, but seemed to be without bones. They were flexible, like the appendices of an octopus. So was the rest of her body.

Her skin was pure white.

His gaze dropped to the dark spot between her legs. What he had perceived as thick hair was nothing but a large mass of wriggling tendrils surrounding the swollen ridge of an orifice.

Her vagina.

"How did you do it?" he croaked. "With the drug?"

"We don't need drugs." She chuckled. A sound so utterly human. "The drug just makes you more pliable, but most importantly, it sustains your body with strength and staying power."

She smiled. He could tell by the wrinkles around her eyes. "We don't even need that silly little creature, the Mongo. It only makes us lose some control."

"But how? Tell me how?"

"It's Par. She has a special gift. Let us show you."

The form of the feline wavered, blurred, and then he looked at the beautiful young woman he had known so intimately.

The woman on the divan beside her was just as beautiful, but somehow he could not focus his attention on her. His eyes were drawn to the young woman on the floor. She yawned, and then she smiled, transforming her face into a thing of such beauty it made his mind reel.

Then she beckoned. *Come.*

The ghostly touch lasted only a fleeting moment.

He groaned and walked toward her.

The other woman handed him something. "Here," she crooned. "Drink this. It will help."

Without conscious thought, he emptied the offered goblet.

"Par likes what you did with her. You've made her feel good. She wants you again."

A moment of sanity seemed to return to Orion. "No," he moaned. "I must not."

"Oh, yes, you must and you will." The woman laughed, her hand touched his painfully rigid penis, stroked it slowly. "You will," she whispered in his ear. "Because you want to."

He sank to his knees, mounted the young woman who presented her lovely buttocks. Frantically stabbing, he searched for the waiting entrance. "Let me help," the woman whispered. "Remember, she likes it slow." Her hand guided him, moved the pulsing head against the soft entrance of Par's vagina. Then she pressed against him from behind.

He moaned loudly when he felt the tight but oh-so-soft walls closing around his shaft. A satisfied growl joined his loud moan. It seemed to clear his mind for a moment and he fought the illusion.

Kneeling on the rug, he found his hands clamped around the haunches of a sleek-furred giant cat, his member buried to the root in its sexual organ.

He didn't see a tail, just a pair of almost human-like buttocks, covered with short, light brown fur.

The insane lust dropped away, was replaced by anger. He pulled out, swung around. Behind him knelt a white-skinned creature, female, judging by the two breasts. The tiny tendrils around her mouth moved with a life of their own.

"You're strong," the creature said. She moved to a low table, fished something out of a glass jar. Her hands were busy between her legs.

He fought the sudden impulses that assaulted his mind.

Fought and lost.

The power of illusion from the cat-creature and the impulses of the Mongo proved too strong. He moved into the woman's welcoming arms. Her thighs wrapped around his body in an impossible way. His rigid pole found the entrance to her sexual orifice and his mind entered delirium.

It was better than the first time.

Somehow, deep inside him, the alien presence, that thing that made him not human, didn't really care about the physical form of his female partners.

They were only bodies.

Therefore, he plunged his pulsing member over and over into the sucking sheath. When he climaxed, the woman held him to her, kissing him feverishly.

Then she urged him to mount Par again, and he didn't protest.

The lovely illusory body of the young woman underneath him quivered deliciously when his stiff member entered her and, following the whispered instructions of the other woman, he moved at a slow and steady pace.

His hands searched for Par's breast's, and when he found the soft swollen mounds of flesh it never entered his mind he might only be holding on to tufts of soft fur.

The young woman's buttocks worked feverishly as he climaxed inside her hot, almost burning tightness, the only thing that was not an illusion.

"Come," the woman coaxed as he pulled out of Par's sex-organ. "Come." She stretched out on the rug. Her mouth covered his body with kisses. She moved down to his belly and caressed the tip of his penis with her lips. Then, slowly, she sucked the swollen pole into her mouth.

He felt her tongue flicking over the glans. He closed his eyes and let her tongue him to another climax. Her mouth was tight around his shaft, almost like a vagina. When he climaxed, she greedily sucked him dry and swallowed the warm liquid.

Smiling, she released him and gave him another drink. "It is good," she whispered. After a short rest, she mounted him again. He never questioned how her legs and body could be put into such impossible angles. She writhed above him with serpent-like motions. A silent hiss came from her open mouth when he climaxed again.

She kissed him deeply. "We must not forget about Par," she whispered, beckoning toward the young woman who had been watching.

This time Par mounted him as he lay on his back.

At first, she moved slowly on top of him, but after a while, she increased her tempo. Soon her body was just a blur of motion. The pleasure, when he climaxed, was so exquisite and intense, he would have screamed had the other woman not covered his mouth with her own.

When Par slid off him, the woman laughed. "Sometimes she likes it fast," she said, mounting him again. "And so do I," she chuckled, speeding up the motion of her body.

A human woman would not have been able to move with the speed she churned above him. Only the drug and the Mongo made it possible for Orion to endure his rape, because that's what it was, and he didn't mind at all.

Time went by. Orion kept pumping without tiring. He pulled out of the woman's love-channel and pushed his pulsing member into the waiting, slippery sheath of Par. Most of the time he took her from the rear, which seemed to be her favorite position. The only other way with her was for her to be on top, straddling him.

The woman on the other hand seemed to be trying out every possible position. He lay on his back, watching his penis disappear between her buttocks as she slowly lowered herself. The folds of her alien vagina closed greedily around his shaft. His hands stroked her smooth back, her round white buttocks.

Then, without missing a stroke, she pivoted and faced him. Smiling, she took his hands and moved them to her breasts.

At one time, while the woman rode him, Par squatted above him, her vagina touching his face. He pushed his tongue inside. She whined softly and pressed down. She tasted salty, but not unpleasant, and he licked and sucked until she clamped her thighs around his face, shaking violently.

He managed to have his own climax at the same time and felt the woman's vice-like grip as he erupted inside her.

They took rests at frequent intervals. The woman gave him liquids laced with vitamins and drugs. Then she or Par would mount him again. Sometimes, he started with Par, made a few deep strokes, and then he straddled the woman, moved back to Par, back to the woman, and finally climaxed inside Par.

At other times, he'd take the woman first, and then he'd plunge into Par's anticipating pussy, brought her to her climax and finished with the woman.

One time, while he pounded against Par's buttocks, the woman straddled her and presented her steaming vagina to let his tongue enter her deeply. She squirmed and moaned, her hands grasped the root of his penis and controlled his speed as he moved back and forth between Par's buttocks.

Finally, all three of them collapsed into a tangled heap, their limbs entwined in each other. Orion's penis was still inside the woman's vagina, but he had made his last stroke for a while.

Her head rested between Par's legs where her tongue had been active, but now she just lay there, breathing hard, her eyes closed.

Thank you. You've made me very happy.

The ghostly voice whispered inside his head and he heard Par's silvery laughter. In the half-awake state of his mind, he saw her running across a meadow filled with flowers. Part cat-creature, part human girl.

The outside form is not important. The soul is your true self.

She smiled and kissed him with red, human lips. Her yellow eyes stared into his. Then she turned and bounded away.

He was still dazed and exhausted when he awoke. Looking around, he found himself alone. Groaning, he staggered to his feet and searched for his clothing. As he dressed, the door opened and the guard walked in.

"Sure took your time to wake up," the guard said. "I had instructions not to disturb you. Very unusual. Most of the time these people don't give a damn about the slaves." He gave Orion a critical look. "You must have done something very special." He grinned. "I couldn't help but wonder about the noises I heard coming from this suite. Grunting, screaming, hissing, roaring. I figured you'd be just pieces of meat when I saw the big cat. Not that I cared. But now I am curious. What happened in here? Did you fuck them both?"

Orion just looked at him, but said nothing.

Chapter Fourteen

Two nights later Ceana visited him again. He was asleep when she slid under the covers, but he awoke from her touch.

You don't have to make love to me if you don't want to, she said inside his head. *But don't send me away. Just let me lie in your arms.*

He sensed her anxiety, her hunger. *It is all right*. His thought impulses were soothing. He kissed her gently.

You saw what I did. What I had to do. She seemed apologetic.

I saw. I admit I was angry when I watched you and I felt sorry for you.

I don't want your pity, Hektor, just your understanding and maybe a little bit of warmth and affection. She pressed her warm, nude body against his, trembled when his hand ran down her back. *Love me, Hektor,* she pleaded. *Love me now*.

He didn't need any encouragement. Already, he was responding to her caressing hands.

Her breath quickened as he rolled on top of her and her legs opened to welcome his searching pole. With a deep sigh, they slipped together. As their bodies joined, so did their minds.

After his third climax, she chuckled inside his head. *I have wondered about you, Hektor. Isn't it a bit unusual for human male to have so many orgasms in such a short time?*

That is my special gift. He grinned and then he became serious. *It is also my hang-up. I have a tremendous sexual appetite. Sometimes it does interfere with my work.*

Her turned her around, made her kneel, and cupped her thin body. She gasped as he pushed into her. *I have a feeling you're getting ready for another one*. She moaned. Her mind flowed into his. *I'll be sore in the morning*.

She left shortly before dawn, after having slept in his arms for a few short hours.

When it was time for him to rise he felt rested and almost at peace. The day went by quickly. He looked forward to the night.

After work, a guard came and told him to follow. They took the elevator up to another level, where he was taken into a richly decorated suite. As he entered the room, he was surprised to see Sheel. She sat in a large chair before a low table.

"Sit down," she said, pointing to a chair opposite from her.

He followed her invitation and looked at her.

"I have watched you," she said in her husky voice.

"Are there any problems?" he asked.

"No." She smiled strangely, her red eyes studying him. "In fact I am quite pleased with you." Offering him a glass of wine, she leaned forward. She had loosened her coarse black hair and it fell into her face. "Don't worry. The wine is not drugged."

Her smile widened. "I can't blame you for being cautious. After your recent experience, it is understandable."

"I don't quite understand."

"You will, Orion. There is something I want you to see." She pointed at a large screen on the wall. "Watch that."

At her command, the screen sprang to life. Then, after a few specific instructions to the computer, Orion stared at the three-dimensional display of something he seemed to remember, but only vaguely.

He saw a big naked man kneeling behind a large feline. Another humanoid creature with flexible arms and legs clung to him, moving with him as he pushed his swollen member into the sexual organ of the big cat.

A low growl filled the room, accompanied by the grunts of the man and a soft hissing sound, which escaped from the round mouth of the female creature clinging to him.

"What a performance," Sheel commented. "I must admit, you are quite a stud."

"I was drugged," Orion defended himself, "and under the influence of the Mongo. I don't remember much about the whole incident."

"It doesn't matter." Sheel leaned back into her chair. "It is obvious you do have a certain talent."

His gaze followed hers as she studied the screen. He saw himself lying on his back, his rigid mast sticking up straight. The cat-creature straddled him and deftly impaled herself on his pole. A close-up shot in the corner of the screen showed his penis slowly disappear inside the creature's sexual organ.

Par, he remembered her name, moved slowly on top of him. Every time she sank down to take his organ deep into her, she emitted a low growl. Speeding up her rhythmic up and down, her creamy human-like buttocks became almost invisible.

He watched himself climax, not remembering what he witnessed, and he was surprised how cool watching this left him. The man he watched could have been someone else, as far as he was concerned.

He remembered a beautiful girl with lovely breasts, not a cat. Even the other creature who mounted his look-alike and twisted her supple body into impossible positions was a stranger. In his memory, she was a mature woman of exceptional beauty, not a white skinned thing without bones.

However, he knew what he saw was the truth.

He shrugged mentally as her words suddenly popped into his mind.

Does the form really make so much difference?

Those two creatures had been intelligent females. Looking at them now, he had to admit that there was a certain beauty about them. The graceful way they moved, the gentleness the cat-like creature displayed as she carefully mounted him, the tender warm hands of the other 'woman' stroking his body. Letting him rest undisturbed after they finished with him.

They were not beasts but caring beings with warm feelings for other entities, however different they may be.

Sheel's words brought back his attention to the present as she gave new instructions to the computer.

The screen went blank for a moment, and then it sprang back to life.

He groaned when he saw the two naked figures writhing on a bunk

"Ceana has talents also, and even without speech she certainly knows how to express herself. You two seem to communicate quite well." Sheel smiled. "As you can see, there are no secrets here."

"I can see that," he said dryly. "What is the purpose of this? Are you going to punish me?"

"Oh, no." Sheel laughed. "Ceana is free to do what she wants. She isn't a slave."

"How about me?" he asked, lifting his glass.

Putting her own glass to her lips, she took a small sip and looked at him over the rim. The color of her eyes seemed to have deepened.

"Fuck me!" she said.

He almost choked on his drink, shocked at the unexpected turn of events. "What's that?" he said, sputtering.

"I want you to fuck me. Now." Her voice sounded low and

throaty.

"Now?"

"Yes, now."

"I'm not certain if I can make love to you now. I'm very tired."

She leaned back into her cushions. "Who said anything about 'making love'? I want to feel that fat prick of yours inside my cunt. I want you to fill me with your hot discharge." She chuckled. "I have switched off the monitors. Nobody will ever know what happens in my private quarters. It is just you and me."

She stood up, untied the belt around her waist. As the loose robe pooled around her ankles, Orion couldn't help but stare. Her slightly sagging breasts looked small on her large frame, but they were enormous. Thick, black hair covered most of her flat belly. Her swollen pubic mound, two prominent muscles at the juncture of her strong thighs, was completely hairless.

While her body color was a deep purple, the skin around her pubis was as white as snow and her labia blood red.

He noticed something different about her legs. Her muscular thighs were slim and well formed. She seemed double-jointed below her knees, and instead of feet, her legs ended up in hoofs, something he had somehow already suspected.

Smiling, she opened her arms and stepped closer. She moved her hips enticingly in a slow grinding motion.

When her body almost touched his, he became aware of her musky odor, but he didn't find it unpleasant and felt himself responding, like an animal in heat.

"Come on," she said with a throaty purr, opening his shirt. Then she fairly ripped it off him and pushed down his pants. Looking at his growing erection, she knelt in front of him. Her tongue flicked rapidly over the head of his penis, and then her lips closed around it. Greedily, she sucked the entire length of his organ into her mouth.

He closed his eyes, stood without moving, enjoying the exquisite pleasure her tonguing gave him. She seemed to sense when he was at the verge of coming. Squeezing the base of his shaft tightly, she released him.

Then she laid down on her back and spread her legs wide. "Now!" she moaned. It sounded like a growl from deep inside her throat. "Put it into me now!"

He nearly fell on top of her in his eagerness and shoved his rampant prick into her waiting cunt. She felt wet and soft like jelly, but as soon as he entered her, the muscles of her vagina closed tightly around his shaft and his fears that her love-channel might be too large for him were quickly disbursed. To the contrary, she felt almost too tight.

She kissed him hungrily as she met his powerful thrusts. He buried his face between the fleshy mounds of her breasts. Her strong arms crushed him to her and she took the full weight of his heavy body without protest.

Grunting and breathing like an angry beast, he bucked between her muscular, but soft thighs. He felt her hoofs digging into his buttocks, pushing as he thrust into her.

Forgotten was his fatigue. Now there was only the woman underneath him, demanding his full attention.

* * * *

"I know you are capable of multiple orgasms," she moaned, "so don't hold back too long. I want to feel your hot semen gush into my cunt." She moaned again. "I'm ready for it now. Give it to me. Flood me!"

She slammed up against him, the strong muscles of her vagina rippling over his shaft demanding delivery.

He let the floodgates down, rammed brutally into her as deep as he could and felt his discharge shooting from him with explosive force.

Her hoofed feet dug painfully into his buttocks as she pushed against him and her fingers raked his back, drawing blood. Her own orgasm reached its peak and warm liquid made her sheath even more slippery, her inside muscles moved like an independent entity across his bursting member.

She didn't give him a chance to recover and kept right on hammering into him, and it didn't take long before he gushed into her again. After his third climax, he sagged against her. "I must rest for a while," he panted. "You'll kill me if we keep this up."

Chuckling, she released him. As he rolled onto his back, she stood up and walked toward the table. He admired her voluptuous, powerful body. She was a big woman and yet, naked, she appeared almost slim.

Her buttocks were large, but in proportion to the rest of her body; just like her breasts. She moved gracefully and her muscles rippled as she walked silently across the floor.

He closed his eyes for a while and completely relaxed his body.

He knew she wasn't finished with him yet. Her sexual appetite seemed enormous.

When he sensed her near, he opened his eyes to look at her. Smiling, she handed him his glass.

"Here, lover, strengthen yourself."

He emptied the filled glass, felt the potent liquid running down his parched throat.

"I like the smell of wine on my lover's breath," she purred, her own breath hot on his throat.

He felt his body responding. Suddenly, he was strong again. "You tricked me," he murmured. "The wine was drugged. You said no drugs."

"A small lie," she breathed, a smile tucking at her lips. Her eyes glowed red and she sighed deeply as she lowered herself onto his rigid shaft. The red lips of her vagina closed over the swollen head, and he watched as his penis slowly disappeared.

Grunting, he grabbed her wide hips and pushed upward. Her strong fingers curled around his biceps and, moaning deeply, she churned above him.

His eyes fastened on her big breasts as they bobbed up and down. Her nipples were long, thick, and blood red. When he climaxed, her powerful thighs clamped around his hips and she let out a low, keening cry as his hot sperm gushed against the walls of her pulsing sheath.

Her own warm discharge wet his pubic hair as it flowed from her.

She slid off him and knelt on the carpet, her back arched and her buttocks up. "You know what I want," she purred.

He mounted her from the back, put his penis between her fat purple cheeks, felt her soft labia close around his shaft.

"No," she said softly. "Not my cunt."

Chapter Fifteen

He didn't really like doing it that way, but he obliged her. At first, she was extremely tight, but as he slowly pushed, his penis greased from her juices, she worked her buttocks against him. Once lodged inside her anal canal, he began to move slowly back and forth.

His hands went around her thighs and, finding what he was searching, he inserted a finger into her vagina.

"That's good," she moaned loudly, rocking against him. "Oh, that's good."

When he felt his climax approaching, he pulled out quickly and rammed his penis into her dripping, trembling vagina. She cried out as her hot walls closed around his spurting member.

"Ahh, you know exactly what to do," she groaned when she felt his fiery discharge. "Ahh...push...push...now...!" She collapsed, her breath rasping in her throat. "What a stud!" she whispered. Then she turned under him, pulled him between her opening thighs. Her hands grabbed his rigid organ and, with the help of her guiding hands, he sank his pole back into her tight, hot sheath.

"Faster," she screamed, pumping beneath him. "Faster...! Fill me as often as you can."

Each time he rammed deep into her, he could feel the thick muscles of her vulva constricting around the base of his shaft. When he pulled back, those strange muscles stopped him from pulling his swollen head completely out of her. Only when he climaxed, she let up on the pressure.

Again, she cried out as an orgasm shook her body. Opening her eyes, she looked at him, smiling lazily. Then she released him and sat up. "I'll get us something to drink." She got up and walked to a dispenser.

When she came back and handed him the glass, he hesitated.

"Don't worry, no drug this time," she assured him. "Just special vitamins and a mixture of herbs."

As he drank, he studied her. He had to admit, she was beautiful, her body developed to near perfection.

She looked at him from lowered lids. "I admire physical strength," she said, "and you are strong, but you are also smart. You have trained your body and you are in control. The men of my race are capable of multiple orgasms and sexual intercourse is something we treat as highly entertaining, something that must be enjoyed to its fullest potential."

She lay back on the table, her legs spread. "It's been a long time since I had a man like you."

"What about Gror?"

"Gror?" She shrugged. "We have never been involved with each other. There are reasons, which I don't care to discuss." Her legs opened and closed. "Come on," she crooned. "Let's not waste time talking."

He went closer, stood between her widespread legs. The table was just high enough to let his penis touch her sex-organ from a standing position. Taking it deliberately slow, he rubbed the head of his penis against her red labia, tickling her erect clitoris.

"Ahh…" she moaned, closing her strong muscles tightly around the head, capturing him partially inside her. "Don't tease. Push it in all the way…ahh…!"

Slowly, his hips moved forward and his penis disappeared in her hot tunnel. His hands closed over her big breasts, massaging them. He let his eyes feast on her trembling body, admiring the way her flat belly worked as she tried to control herself.

He rocked slowly back and forth between her widespread thighs. Her chest heaved, her breathing quickened. Watching her, he timed his own climax with hers and when he felt it approaching, he slammed into her, his hands clamped around her hips to keep her from sliding off the table.

Then he exploded inside her, spraying the pink walls of her love-channel with his hot sperm. Her hands gripped the edges of the table and her mouth opened to let out a long ecstatic moan.

Her inside muscles milked and sucked until he finished gushing. Then he slipped out of her, his penis limp.

"That was the best one yet," she said, sliding off the table. She lay on the thick carpet, breathing heavily. "Come, lie down beside me. It is time we both got some rest."

He didn't argue and slumped onto the floor. Sighing, he closed his eyes and drifted into a deep sleep.

* * * *

He awoke to find her fondling him.

"Awake?" She smiled, and then she bent to kiss the head of his swelling member. "It's morning. We've slept for hours." She mounted him, and before he realized it, his rigid penis slid into her slippery vagina.

"Let us start the day right and then we'll have breakfast."

She rode him to a shattering climax.

After eating, they had intercourse again. They spent most of the day in various positions, locked together. Sometimes, they ate and drank, without drawing apart. She'd be on her knees, a plate with food in front of her. Orion knelt behind her, his penis lodged deeply inside her vagina, his hips barely moving. On the low table beside him, stood a plate filled with morsels of food.

Alternatively, they would sit on the floor, his rigid pole captured between her legs. While she put food into his mouth, her vagina pulsed around his penis. She had the ability to move the inside muscles of her vagina without moving any other parts of her body. Her double-jointed legs locked around his lower torso, pressing him to her in a tight embrace.

By evening, they both fell into an exhausted sleep.

The next morning he found her sitting at the table, dressed in her black cloak. She sounded cool and aloof when she spoke. "I want you to keep silent about the things we did, do you understand?"

He nodded, smiling dryly. "I understand. Will you need my services again?"

"Perhaps," she said, fingering her whip. "Maybe the next time we will try something different. It all depends on what mood I am in."

* * * *

She called him again, but they never spent as much time together as they did the first time. While they were together, she was passionate, insatiable. In the mine she hardly spoke to him, treated him just like any other slave.

"Why don't you remove my collar?" he asked her, while pounding between her spread thighs.

For an answer, she just laughed, and then she pressed the control band on her wrist, sending a wave of barely noticeable shocks through his body. "Just so you don't forget who is in control," she said. She cried out when he brutally slammed his body against her throbbing vagina.

"You can't hurt me that way." Her breath came in great gasps and her teeth gleamed between her open lips. "It only enhances my pleasure."

With a powerful move, she twisted, put him onto his back. Sitting on top of him and gyrating fiercely, she brought both of them to a powerful climax.

Then she slid off and told him to leave.

One thing puzzled him. She never used a Mongo. Not that he needed it. His pleasure was intense enough without it, and he was consciously aware of their time together. He didn't suffer from lapses of memory.

Ceana came to him on nights when he was not occupied with Sheel. She knew about his involvement with the giantess, but she didn't comment on it. Only once, she told him, "Be careful."

He began to plan his escape.

The next night when Sheel called for him, he had it all worked out.

He took her forcefully from the beginning. Holding back his own orgasms, he made her climax through skillful manipulation. Through trials and errors, he had learned to bring her to a quick orgasm.

"I don't know what you're doing to me today," she moaned, slamming up against him, "but whatever it is, don't stop."

His strength was beginning to wane, but he knew she was almost at the point of exhaustion, too. Finally, when he thought he couldn't hold back any longer, she collapsed under him and murmured, "Enough for a while. I must rest."

Breathing hard, he lay beside her and went into a state of complete relaxation. When he thought he had sufficiently recovered, he opened his eyes and found Sheel in a deep sleep. Carefully, he slid off the bed and on silent feet, he walked through the door into the next room.

He needed different clothing, credits, and some way to get past the controls. Searching through a closet, he picked up one of Sheel's cloaks. Not a perfect disguise, but better than his present outfit.

Just as he put the cloak around his shoulders, her low voice spoke to him from the open door. "Going somewhere?"

He turned around slowly. In the dim light, her purple skin appeared black and her teeth shone white between her smiling lips.

"You exhausted me today and I wanted to get back into my own bed. I need the rest," he said smoothly.

"Is there something wrong with your own clothing?" Her voice sounded dangerously low and her eyes burned red.

He grinned. "You probably won't believe me, but I was curious to see how I looked in this cloak."

"You're right," she said. "I don't believe you." She stood wide-legged. He noticed that she held her right arm behind her back. "You'll never get out alive, Orion. Face it, you're here to stay."

She brought her arm around, fingered the whip in her hand. "Somehow, I knew you would try this one day."

He spread his hands, slowly walking toward her. "I guess you saw right through me."

She lifted the whip and flicked the tip of the lash across his belly. He winced, looking at the broken skin. Then, without warning, he charged her. His body smashed into hers and they both crashed to the floor.

As they rolled on the carped, he forced her legs open and held down her hands.

"You're a beast," she moaned when she felt his penis rubbing against her labia. His penis grew even more and he forced himself into her.

Sighing, she wrapped her legs around his torso. "You've made me angry, but I forgive you." She cried out when she felt his discharge.

"Let's do it the way you like," he said, turning her over.

"Let's," she moaned, arching her back and pushing her buttocks into his groin. Her red-rimmed vagina swallowed him. "Ah, that feels so good."

He hammered into her buttocks with grim determination, and when she clawed at the rug in the throes of a shattering orgasm, he hit her hard at the base of the neck.

She collapsed without a sound.

"Sorry," he murmured, meaning it. "This was necessary." He looked for something he could use to tie her up. His eyes fell on the whip. He took it and tied her arms and legs together behind her back.

The slight hissing of the opening outer door made him jump up and step into the small alcove beside the door. He kept his mind closed for fear of betraying his presence He heard the soft footsteps of someone walking across the thick carpet. The light brightened as the person walked into the room.

Come out, Hektor, she said inside his head and turned toward him.

"Ceana," he said aloud, "You've come at a bad time."

No. She shook her head. *This is the right time. I knew what you were planning. It was clearly in your mind the last time we made love.*

"You're better than I would have guessed." He grinned. "What are you going to do?"

She came close to him and touched his cheek. *I want to help you.*
"Why?"

*Because I am very fond of you. You never looked upon me as
some kind of freak or outsider. You are a good person, Hektor.* She
put her arms around his neck and kissed him. *You'll never make it
without me.* Then she looked at Sheel. *Is she all right?*

He nodded. "I didn't hit her too hard. She'll wake up with a
terrific headache, that's all."

She let go of him and went to search for something, seemed to
have found it in a small compartment beside Sheel's bed. She bent
down beside the giantess and pressed her hand against her neck. This
will keep her under for about six hours, she explained. Enough time
for you to get away.

Looking at him with a strange smile, she began to shed her
clothing. Naked, she lay down on the bed, her legs slightly spread.
For the first time, he saw her nude body close in bright light. As he
already knew, her pubic area was completely hairless. Looking
between her legs seemed like seeing the smooth vagina of a young
girl, but she was not young.

*We have one hour. Make love to me and make me happy once
more.*

He shrugged the cloak from his shoulders and joined her on the
wide bed. Her body was soft and responding as his hands stroked her
tenderly. His finger touched the moistness between her legs and he
knew she was ready for him. With a deep sigh, she opened her legs
wide and let him enter.

Again, their minds blended, and, gently, they climbed together
toward the peak of their passion. When they were finished, she cried
softly against his shoulder.

Wiping the tears from her lovely face, he smiled and looked into
her eyes.

I love you. Her voice sounded like a soft whisper inside his mind.
*I didn't want to fall in love with you, but I did. I know you must leave
and I must stay.* Taking his head between her hands, she kissed him
tenderly. *Thank you for the wonderful hours you gave me. I will
always cherish them.*

She twisted away from him. *Time to go. Let's hurry now.*

She dressed quickly and then she walked over to the computer
terminal. Come on, Hektor, we'll have to program you into the

computer, but first... She produced an electronic key and pressed it against his collar. With a gentle click, it opened up, and she removed it from his neck.

"That's feels so much better." Orion rubbed his neck, and then he put a skullcap, which was connected to the computer, on his head.

Ceana manipulated a keyboard under the terminal. *This is only a temporary pass,* she said, *but it will be good enough.*

Wearing the cloak, he followed her down the empty corridor. She took him into the outfitting room, where she gave him a guard's uniform.

Dressed like that, he felt much better and more confident that he would succeed.

You look handsome in that uniform. Ceana giggled inside his head. *Too bad, there is so little time left. I might ravish you right here.*

"You would, wouldn't you?" He grinned. "Don't you have that backwards? Isn't it usually the men who do the ravishing?"

Not where I come from.

"Interesting place," he joked, still grinning. "Maybe some day I'll have to come and visit there."

Oh, you. She smiled, but he saw the moisture in her eyes.

She came close and held onto him. *I wish we could have met under different circumstances.* She let go and took his arm. *Get moving.*

Down the corridor, they walked again. So far, they had not met anyone. As they stepped into the elevator, they found only one person in it. Another guard. He threw them only a short glance, but didn't pay them any attention.

When the elevator stopped, they left and quickly walked down another corridor, which led into a vast cavern. It was a hangar. Men and machines were busy unloading crates from large transporters.

"This is where we part, Hektor. One of those transporters will leave shortly for North-City. I don't know which one. You'll have to find that out for yourself. You're on your own."

It was easy enough to get to this point, he said in mind speech. *Much easier than I anticipated.*

Don't be lulled into false security, Hektor. We have been scanned many times. Without the programming, you would have been caught as soon as you stepped into the elevator.

Thank you, Ceana. I wish I could give you something in return. He stepped closer to kiss her, but she put a hand against his chest.

No, we may be watched. Her pale eyes misted. *Good-bye, my love. And good luck.*

She turned and, briskly, she walked away. He looked after her with mixed feelings. He didn't love her, but he had grown fond of her. Intercourse with her had changed from mere animalistic coupling to something that was close to love. Not just satisfaction of lust, as had been the case with Sheel.

Shrugging, he headed toward one of the loading docks, where a number of men were milling around, apparently waiting for something.

One of the men, a guard with a weapon carelessly slung across his forearm, looked up as he approached.

"Which transporter goes to North-City?" Orion asked him.

The guard scrutinized him for a moment. Orion tensed, his hand itching to reach for his own weapon.

"We have a comedian here," the guard said. Then he pointed to the group of waiting men. "Just get in line. We're almost ready to board."

Chapter Sixteen

The snow-covered mountains lay below them. Above, the sun was small and far away in a cloudless sky. Listening to the conversations of the other men, Orion tried to relax as much as possible. He felt exhausted from the long fierce night with Sheel and the lack of sleep. His body cried out for rest.

The trip to North-City would not be long. A little over three hours, but they would be three long hours. Although everything had gone smoothly until now, he did not feel safe. He hoped that Sheel would stay out of action until the transporter landed.

If she should wake or somebody discovered her unconscious, he could be in trouble. It wouldn't be hard to figure out which way he had gone.

"Eh, buddy, you haven't said a word since you joined us."

Orion opened his eyes to look at the man who had spoken to him. Tall and lean, with a bushy mustache in his narrow face, the speaker stared at Orion with penetrating eyes.

"Sorry, friend," Orion mumbled. "Don't mean to be unsociable. The truth is I'm quite tired."

"Tired? Doing what?" The other one laughed. "Most of us are looking forward to some tiring action." He poked Orion. "You know what I mean."

Orion grinned. "I know. Looking forward to that myself."

One of the others studied Orion. "Why are you still dressed in your uniform? Might run into trouble in the city."

"Why?" Orion felt himself go tense again.

The others grinned. "You must be new. This your first time off?" the one with the mustache asked.

Orion nodded. "Yeah. And it's about time."

"What level are you in? Never seen you before."

"Level? Ah…" Orion hesitated. "I'm in Section fourteen."

"That far down? You poor bastard. Been there only once." The speaker wiped his forehead on a mock gesture. "Damn hot and sticky down there. That's Gror's territory. They got mostly criminals there."

"You must know Sheel then," another one said. He grinned knowingly at the others. "Giant of a woman. Same species as Gror, except she's got no horns."

121

"The one with the whip? I saw her in the arena."

"That's the one. Nobody knows what she looks like underneath that cloak, but I've heard stories from slaves. She's supposed to have a real hairy, huge cunt with a bunch of muscles inside. Apparently, she fucked this guy to death not so long ago. Ripped his penis right off him with her cunt when he tried to pull out."

"Why would she do that?"

The other one shrugged. "How should I know? She's crazy about fucking and I guess the guy didn't satisfy her."

They all looked at Orion. "You must know her. Can you enlighten us?"

Orion smiled and shrugged. "She's big and mean. Likes to use her whip. That's all I know."

"Hey, what's your name?" the one with the mustache asked. "I'm Bral."

"Orion." He touched Bral's outstretched hand.

Bral scrutinized him, his penetrating eyes narrow. "You know, you look familiar."

"Could be," Orion said, acting nonchalant. "I have that kind of face."

"It will come to me," Bral said. "Don't worry."

"Oh, I won't." Orion pulled his cap deeper into his face. He had recognized Bral the moment he saw him. He was the guard who had taken him from the arena to the suite of the two alien females.

Orion had one thing in his favor. Bral had never heard his voice.

"Tell me something, Bral. Why did the guard back in the hangar carry that heavy hardware? He acted as if he was going to blow me away at any moment."

Bral stared at him. "Are you for real or are you just acting stupid?"

"Remember, I'm new around here."

"Yeah, you told me. I guess there is a reason why they put you down below into Section fourteen."

"Well, are you going to tell me?"

"Don't keep the man in suspense," one of the others laughed. "Tell him already, Bral."

"It's no big secret, really," Bral said. "Lately, we've been having problems with Mongo-hunters. They come in with a bunch of Mongos and then they try to smuggle them out of here without leaving the Company's cut."

"The Company's cut?"

Bral shook his head. "You really don't know, do you? The Hunters use our facilities, rent our skimmers, and then they try to cheat us. Just the other day, one of them lost his skimmer, blamed it on the natives."

"What was his name? Do you know?"

"I don't know. He had this native girl with him. She was real cute, quite young. He kept her in a room, all doped up, a Mongo between her legs. Some of the guys screwed her. I didn't. He wanted too much money for just one lousy piece of tail."

Bral stroked his bushy mustache. "She was quite a looker, though. Had the most beautiful eyes. Real bright."

Brighteyes, Orion thought, anger welling up inside him. "So, what happened?" he asked, keeping his voice steady.

"Oh, well, he skipped without paying for the good time he had here. Stole a skimmer and disappeared."

"But, that's not all of it, is it?" Orion asked.

"Aha, we are finally making a bright deduction." Bral chuckled, lifting his finger in the manner of a lecturer. "No, that is not all. In our laboratories, they have developed a device that enables the wearer to neutralize the effects of the Mongo. This guy I told you about, it is assumed that he also managed to steal one of those devices."

"I suppose that explains the armed guard," Orion commented, and then, venturing a guess, "That device is still in the experimental stage, I assume. Not yet ready for mass production? Also, probably illegal, like the hunting of Mongos?"

Orion saw the flicker of respect in Bral's eyes. "I have a feeling you're not as dumb as you act, my friend. You are correct, of course."

Orion grinned. "And I have a feeling you're not just a regular guard. You know too much."

It was Bral's turn to grin. "Right again. I'm not, as you put it, just a regular guard. I am a Special Officer for GESCOM, responsible for the well-being and safety of our guests. Part of my duties involves safeguarding Company secrets."

"An important man," Orion said dryly, a smile tucking on his lips.

Bral laughed and leaned back. "You're okay, pal. Maybe a little different from the other boys, but that'll change." He closed his eyes. "Yeah, in time you will be just like them."

Orion couldn't miss the sarcasm in Brak's voice. Somehow, he liked the man.

* * * *

They arrived in North-City a couple of hours later and Orion breathed easier when he stepped off the transporter and boarded the shuttle into the domed city.

"Coming with us?" one of his new comrades asked him after leaving the shuttle.

He shook his head. "I've got something important to take care of. Maybe I'll bump into you guys later."

He decided against going back to the hotel he had checked into after arriving on Bakker's Planet, even though the room was his as long as he stayed on the planet.

Before he took a room in another hotel, he went to buy some clothes for himself. He threw the uniform into a public garbage disposal unit, but he kept the gun.

The room was not impressive, the bed not too comfortable, but it was paradise for him. He slept for a long time, deep and untroubled.

* * * *

Locating Storm did not prove to be difficult. Orion gave the directory computer a description of the man and soon the screen displayed his address.

Had Storm only been a visitor, finding him would not have been quite so easy.

After studying a plan of the city on the screen, Orion took a Robotaxi. He got off a couple of blocks from his destination and walked the rest of the way. The building Storm stayed in looked quite shabby from the outside. Some of the plastic imitation stone front needed replacing.

The entrance to the building was not controlled electronically. An old guy sat inside a little booth and looked sleepily at Orion.

Orion slipped him a few credit notes. "I'd like to surprise a friend," he grinned. "So do me a favor and don't announce me."

The old man stuffed the money into a dirty shirt pocket and gave him a toothless grin. "I didn't see you. By the way, the elevator is out of order. You'll have to use the stairs."

"Thanks." Orion headed for the stairs.

Storm lived on the fourth floor. The door to his suite was locked. Orion mentally scanned the rooms behind the door and sensed the presence of two people. He pressed an electronic override against the lock and, with a barely audible click, the bolt slipped back. Carefully, he pushed the door open and sneaked into the room.

Stepping into a dimly lit kitchenette, he silently walked across the smooth floor and into a larger living room. On the worn-out carpet on the floor, he saw a pair of large, naked buttocks hammering between two fleshy, widespread thighs.

Storm's heavy breathing and the loud moans of the woman filled the room. Orion watched them for a few minutes, and then, as Storm's buttocks began to quiver, he stepped closer and put his foot on the man's back.

"What the hell!" Storm yelled in surprise. Then he tried to roll off the woman, but Orion pushed harder.

The woman cried out, as the heavy body of Storm began squeezing the breath from her lungs.

"Finish up and enjoy it," Orion said coldly. "This might be your last piece of tail."

"You!" Storm cursed, craning his neck.

Orion stepped back and let the heavyset man get off the woman. Orion noticed that she was just an adult girl.

"You still like them young, I see," he said. "Do older women intimidate you?"

Storm threw himself against Orion's legs. Expecting the attack, Orion evaded him easily, and then he kicked Storm in the face with his booted foot.

Letting out a hoarse yell, Storm fell backwards, his hand covering his nose.

"That is just a down payment," Orion said harshly. "Where is the girl you abducted?"

Storm spat blood. "You'll never know, you bastard." The blood from his ruined nose ran down his hairy chest. Again, he charged Orion, his eyes bloodshot.

Stepping aside easily, Orion grabbed his bull neck and rammed him into the wall. Dazed, Storm fell to the floor, where he lay breathing hard, his blood staining the dirty carpet.

Grabbing him by the hair, Orion pulled back his head. "Tell me where the woman is or I'll break your fucking neck!"

"Fuck you!" Storm cursed him.

Orion gave his neck a slight twist. Storm struggled to get up, but he was too weak.

"Now!" Orion demanded.

"Alright, I'll talk. Just let me sit up."

"No tricks." Orion let go of him and stood, waiting.

The girl lay on the floor, petrified with fear, her legs still spread. She was a little on the plump side, but not bad looking. Her big breasts sagged on either side of her ribcage.

"You can close your legs now," Orion said, grinning. "I believe your lover is finished for today and I am not in the mood."

"You've broken my nose," Storm complained, breathing harshly through his mouth.

"I know. I did that on purpose, but you'll live. For now."

"What do you mean by *for now*?"

"It all depends on how I like your answers. So start talking."

"I've sold her."

"Sold her? Explain."

"What's there to explain? She's gone. You might as well forget about her. What is she to you anyway?"

Orion looked at him sharply. "Who bought her and what is she doing?"

Storm managed a strained laugh. "She's doing what she knows best. What all these native girls know how to do best. As to who owns her now? You don't want to mess with these people."

"Don't worry about that. Just give me a name."

"It's your funeral. His name is 'S'. That's all I know."

"S," Orion repeated. "That doesn't tell me much, but it's a start. Where do I find this mysterious 'S'?"

"You don't find him, but the girl is at the *Lair of the nine Serpents*. They might even let you in if you can afford the delights waiting for you inside."

"Who is this Mr. 'S'? What shady business is he involved in?"

"You've said it," Storm growled. "Shady business—Mongos, slaves, whores, murder. You name it." He winced when his fingers probed his nose. "I hope they cut off your balls, you bastard!"

Orion gave him an icy stare. "Count yourself lucky that I have certain scruples. I should kill you for what you did to me and to that sweet innocent girl." He paused as his scanning mind picked up the thought impulses of someone coming up the stairs. "It seems the decision what to do with you has been taken out of my hands."

He turned when he heard the footsteps of the person walking through the open door and said, "Welcome to the party, Bral. As you see, I've beaten you to him. He's all yours."

The tall man with the bushy mustache grimaced, the gun in his hand aimed at Orion's chest. "Hello, Orion. Why am I not happy to see you?"

Orion shrugged. "How should I know? This is the man, though, that you want, not me."

"I'm not sure, Orion. You see, I remembered where I saw you."

"Good for you, Bral. Like I said, this is the man you are looking for. He is responsible for putting me where you saw me. Besides, we are on equal grounds here. I don't have a collar around me neck. Don't try to be a hero." His last words carried an unmistakable warning. Bral would be a fool to miss and ignore them.

The tall man walked into the living room, looked at the girl on the floor and then at Orion. "Caught him with your girl?" He grinned. "At least she's human."

His words seemed to bring the female out of her shocked state. "I'm nobody's girl. Not his and not his." She stood up and began dressing. "Just let me out of this madhouse."

Bral pointed his gun at her. "Sit down, girl. You'll leave when I tell you so."

He sat down, his gun casually in his lap. "I knew there was something weird about you, Orion. I don't know what I should do with you; after all, you are an escaped criminal. Maybe even a very dangerous one. Just look at what you did to Storm."

"I thought you didn't know his name?"

"I lied." Bral smiled. "Just like you."

"I had a better reason," Orion said. "Maybe you'd like to hear it."

Chapter Seventeen

The *Lair of the nine Serpents* was as he had suspected. He had seen places like that on many planets. They were always the same. Only the name changed.

Inside, the place lay in semi-darkness. Behind a counter, sat a female with a painted face. Her ample bosom left nothing for the imagination. He also saw the burly men, casually leaning against the bar, their eyes watching the entrance.

He didn't see anyone else in the place.

"Anyone special you're looking for?" the woman asked with a big smile.

"Depends." He grinned. "A friend sent me. His name is Storm."

"Storm," the girl repeated, a momentary glazed look in her hazel eyes. Orion knew she was connected to a monitor and waited for an answer to confirm the name.

She smiled. "Oh, yes. Mr. Storm. You say he's a friend of yours?"

"I didn't say *a good friend*. Let's just say we had dealings together, you understand?"

"I understand." She nodded, gave him an inquiring look. "What did Mr. Storm recommend?"

"Well…" Orion hesitated. "He told me about this native girl who is in your…ah…employment because of him. She has real bright eyes and," he winked slyly, "certain other traits."

"I see." She pushed a button underneath the counter.

Another girl came out of an alcove and smiled at him. "This way, sir."

He followed her through a curtain-covered doorway into another room. Behind a large desk, sat a fat man. Orion detected a thought-scrambler hidden inside an amulet hanging from a golden chain around his thick neck.

"Leave your gun here," he told Orion. "No weapons allowed beyond this point." His little eyes trailed Orion's clothing. "The female you want is new. Very special. Very expensive."

"Name the price. I can pay."

"One hundred credits. Cash. One hour. If you want a Mongo between her legs it'll cost you double."

Orion grinned. "You're right, that is expensive. I'll take it. No Mongo, though. I want to know what I'm doing. If she is as good as you say I won't need one of those little critters."

He put the money and his gun on the desk. Smiling, he said, "I hope she's worth it. If she isn't I'll have one less friend."

The fat man smiled thinly. "Storm doesn't keep friends for very long. But be assured, this time he didn't lie to you."

Orion tipped an imaginary hat and followed the girl down a thickly carpeted corridor. She stopped beside a door and opened the lock with an electronic key. "I'll be back in an hour," she said, giving him a long look. "No rough stuff in there, okay? My employer likes to keep his merchandise for a while." She hesitated. "I've never seen you here before."

He laughed. "That's because I've never been here before. What's your name?"

"Tessma," she said, smiling up at him. "If you feel like company after you're through with her, I could be available."

"We'll see, Tessma." Orion looked after her as she walked away from him, her hips swaying. She turned once to look back, aware that he was watching her.

He chuckled and walked through the door.

Brighteyes was there. She lay naked on a wide bed, apparently asleep. When he touched her shoulder, she turned around and lazily smiled up at him. Her shiny eyes had a glazed look and he knew she was drugged.

She opened her arms and pulled him down on top of her, kissing him hungrily. Her legs wrapped around his lower torso and her hips moved against him.

Knowing that his every move was being monitored, he had to go through with the act.

"Easy, girl," he muttered. "Let me take off my pants first." He pushed them past his hips and pulled them off his feet.

She moaned, her fingers curled around his growing erection, and then she practically forced herself onto his rigid shaft.

He hated what he was doing and was angry with the people who were responsible for the way he had to use this lovely young woman. She didn't recognize him. To her he was just another stranger. Drugged with a strong aphrodisiac she wanted nothing more but fuck. With anyone who came into her room.

He detected a small, flesh colored disk attached to her forehead, a

129

device that received impulses from a computer and transmitted them to her brain, causing her mind to live in a world of fantasy.

He had to get her out of here, but he didn't know how.

For one hour, she plunged underneath him, crying out once in awhile as she experienced an orgasm. When the hour was over, she suddenly seemed to loose interest in him. She pushed him off and turned away.

This action confirmed his suspicion that they had been watched closely and that she was under the complete control of a computer. No more than a pleasure robot.

The door opened and Tessma entered. She looked at his half-erect penis, licking her lips. Beneath her semi-transparent blouse, he could see her breasts rise and fall. "You are a gentle lover," she said.

"How would you know?" he asked, reaching for his pants.

She came closer. "I was at the monitor."

"You were watching us? You're a voyeur."

She laughed haughtily. "Don't be a fool. It's part of my job. You don't really believe we let strangers do what they want with the girls. Some men have strange appetites." Her hands traveled over his body, touched his stomach.

"Who is watching now?" He grasped her hands.

She gasped as he pulled her close. "Nobody, I swear." Her eyes were pleading. "Most men who come in here are nothing but animals. Filth. But you...you seem different."

"Different enough to get it for free?" He smiled and then he kissed her.

She returned his kiss. When they drew apart, she looked at him with hunger in her eyes. "Yes, for free," she breathed. "But not here."

She took his hand and drew him out of the room. He threw one more glance at Brighteyes who lay curled up on the bed. She looked so peaceful. Just a lovely, nude young woman with an innocent smile on her lips.

I'll get you out of here. Somehow, I'll find a way.

In a way, it was too bad that his hands were tied more or less, where Storm was concerned. Bral had put his claim on him in the name of GESCOM.

Tessma led him into another room, not much different from the one Brigheyes lay in.

"Come on," she coaxed. "I can't wait."

She undressed slowly in front of him, exposing a nicely formed body with wide hips and a narrow waist. Her breasts were not very large, just big enough to give them a slight sag. Below her flat belly, a thick triangle of auburn hair confirmed that it was her true color.

He put a hand over one of her breasts and squeezed lightly. She moaned. Her arms went around his neck, pulling him on top of her as she slid to the thickly carpeted floor.

Then her long legs opened wide and his rigid pole found her moist cleft. She sighed heavily as he eased into her.

"You are a big man," she breathed. "In many ways."

"So I've been told." Grinning, he started a slow and steady rhythm. When her first orgasm shook her, he flooded her sucking love channel with his own discharge, making her cry out. He had not climaxed with Brighteyes and making love to this woman brought welcome relieve and great enjoyment. Especially, since she gave herself freely. After his third climax, he pulled out and rolled onto his back. "I'm giving up. You are too much woman for me, Tessma."

She giggled, trying to catch her breath beside him. "Who are you kidding," she said. "Maybe next time I'll call one of the other girls to help me out."

"I'm not paying extra." He chuckled and looked at her. "It seems you enjoy your work."

Her eyes were quite serious, even though her lips smiled. "I am luckier than most of the other girls, because I enjoy what I'm doing. Also, the fat man behind the front desk? He is my brother. That allows me certain privileges."

"Why does your brother let you do this kind of work?"

He sensed her sudden anger. "What's wrong with this work?"

"Nothing," he said soothingly. "It's just…aren't you afraid you might end up like that native girl. Even a blind man can see that she is full of drugs."

"I'll never end up like her." She gave him a calculating look. "I don't know you and I'd like to keep it that way. I don't even want to know what kind of business you're in. Better for both of us. You seem like an all right guy. I'm certain you are not stupid and you know that the girl you were with is not here of her own choice. She was bought. You also know who sold her to us."

"To us?"

"Just a figure of speech." She shook her head. "I have nothing to do with that."

"Who does?"

"None of your business."

"Maybe it is. What about 'S'? I understand he owns this place."

She tensed and shot him a quick glance, and then she looked away. Suddenly, she seemed afraid. "Who the hell are you? Why all these questions?"

He laughed and stroked her breast. "Just curious. I might possibly have business with him." His finger trailed across her stomach, down to her fluffy triangle. Toying with the auburn hair, he asked, "Ready again?"

"I'm not in the mood anymore." Her body had gone rigid. He felt her shivering, even though it was warm in the room.

"Is it something I said? I apologize if I upset you. Didn't mean to."

"Are you working for him?" She stared at him, fear in her blue green eyes.

"Who? 'S'?" He chuckled when she silently nodded. "No, I'm not working for him. I don't even know who the man is."

"Better you don't," she murmured, still looking at him. "I might be wrong, but you don't seem to be the kind of guy who would be mixed up in that type of business. Be careful and don't ask too many questions."

Shivering, she snuggled against him. "I'm cold," she whispered. "Make me hot."

Chapter Eighteen

He went back twice, asking and paying for Brighteyes. Both times, Tessma entertained him after…for free. The third time he went, he asked for Tessma.

"Tessma?" The fat man looked at him. "She is not one of the regular girls. I doubt if she'll want you."

So he didn't know about his sister and Orion. A fact that raised some questions.

Orion grinned. "I thought a change might do me some good."

"If you want change, we have other girls. How about something exotic, like a girl from the Lira System, with four breasts. Or how would you like to have one with two vaginas?"

"No, thank you. I've changed my mind." Orion put the cash on the desk. "I'm actually quite satisfied with my choice. Same girl."

The fat man chuckled. "As long as she satisfies your sexual hunger. You must be starved for sex, but that is not my business."

"You're right," Orion said. "It is not your business."

The fat man put the money away. "If you pay, you're welcome here, my friend. Let's hope your money lasts as long as your hunger. Actually, the girl is busy with another customer at the moment. After that, she'll be bathed. That means you'll have to wait."

"I'll wait."

He rang for Tessma, who came in smiling.

"It'll be at least another hour before she's free," she informed him in the corridor. "How do you plan to spend the time?"

He gave a wide grin. "How do you think?"

Smiling, she came into his arms. "I was hoping you'd say that. Let's not waste any time then."

She kept him busy for over an hour and he did his best to give her as many orgasms as possible, without having his own climax. She was hooked on him and a plan began to form in his mind. He saw a way to free Brighteyes from her prison.

"Ahh…" she sighed when he finally pulled out. "You are a master. You seem to know my body like your own and you do the right thing at the right time."

"I admit I do have a certain talent." He smiled. "However, it is you who draws it out of me. A master is nothing without a perfect instrument."

"You even say the right things." She yawned and stretched like a cat. Then she slid off the bed and padded to the lavatory.

He watched the round gloBes of her buttocks move up and down and said, "You have a beautiful ass, you know."

"I know." She laughed and wiggled her behind. "Does it excite you?"

He jumped up and grabbed her from behind, pulling her into his lap. His stiff penis slid between her soft buttocks and caressed the fleshy lips of her vagina.

She gasped when he bent her over a low chair. "I think you should go now," she whispered, her breath quickening. She moved against him and pressed her buttocks into his groin.

"One more time," he grunted, adjusting her hips, and then, with a deep moan, he slid into her already greedily working sheath. His hands grabbed her buttocks and squeezed them hard as he moved in and out of her tight cleft.

She clawed at the chair with her fingers, searching for something to hold.

"Don't stop now," she pleaded and, moaning, she pushed backwards. "Forget about that native girl. I need you more than she does."

Arching her back, she tried to swallow as much of him as she could. Her belly worked feverishly as she bucked underneath him, sliding her well-lubricated sheath over his pulsing member.

"Oh, oh," she wailed, as she felt the sweet torment of another orgasm. His own climax approached and he reached around to take her swinging breasts into his hands. Digging his fingers into their firm flesh, he erupted with great force and let out a suppressed shout the same time she cried out.

They sank to the floor, both of them exhausted and satisfied.

"That was terrific," she said after a while, stirring under him. Then she giggled. "I'm glad you love my ass. I might have missed out on a good fuck."

Chuckling, he slapped her playfully on the rump and rolled onto his back.

She kissed him on the tip of his nose. "Time for you to leave. I don't want my brother to get suspicious."

"Didn't you tell me he has no say over your actions?"

"He hasn't. Not usually, but I'm neglecting my work. Spending too much time with you and leaving the monitors alone for too long. If anything happens and I don't catch it…"

"I get the hint." He laughed and began dressing.

Tessma took him to Brighteyes and waited until he closed the door. As usual, the girl didn't recognize him and he lay in her embrace, without much enthusiasm. Tessma had worn him out and there wasn't much left for Brighteyes. It didn't really matter. The time he spent with Brighteyes was never pleasurable for him, except for the fact that he held her in his arms and tried to fulfill whatever fantasy she played out in her drugged mind.

The next day he made up his mind to go back to his hotel room by the spaceport. Nobody waited for him and when he checked his luggage, it seemed untouched. He didn't find any visible signs of anyone having been in his room while he was gone.

He went downstairs into the hotel's dining room to have a decent meal, and after a couple of drinks, he went back to his room, feeling happy for the moment.

A maid was busy dusting the furniture when he entered.

Looking up, she gave him a friendly smile. She was dark-skinned, with short, white hair. "I'll be only a moment," she said.

Even though he had never seen her before, somehow, she seemed familiar and when her mind touch came, he was only mildly surprised.

Nice to see you again, Hektor. She kept on dusting, while her thoughts poured into his mind. *Don't say anything. This room is monitored. Follow me in a couple of minutes.*

"There, that should do it," she said, and then she walked out of the room.

Orion sat down in a chair, and then, as if thinking of something, he snapped his fingers and left his room again.

She was waiting for him at the end of the corridor.

Follow me upstairs, she sent and took the stairs to the next floor. She opened a door with an electronic key and they both entered the room.

"What is going on, Azalee?" he asked, watching her as she removed the mask from her head.

She shook her long copper-colored hair and smiled. "I've missed you, Hektor," she said, slipping into his arms.

Her lips were warm and soft as she kissed him hungrily. "Let's celebrate our reunion first," she whispered. "There is enough time later to talk."

He nodded and they undressed each other. Then they climbed on top of a big wide bed and lay in each other's arms.

"It's been so long," she moaned as he eased himself into her warm sheath. "I've almost forgotten how good it feels."

Afterwards, she lay beside him, holding his hand. "I guess you're wondering why I never came looking for you?"

"The thought has crossed my mind." He looked into her beautiful face. "Why didn't you?"

"Dr. Kirku told me that you left right after my call. I knew that Azur was taking you into the mountains and then into the caverns. Once inside them, I had no way of locating you, but I knew you were safe."

"After what I've been through I can't really agree with you," he commented dryly.

"Tell me what happened to you in there." She popped herself up on her elbows.

He told her. Not everything. There were a few occasions where he had to edit his story, but he told her almost everything.

"You took part in the fertility rites?" she asked.

Nodding, he smiled. "It was purely scientific. I needed first hand information about what the Mongo can do."

She didn't smile. "Then you know how important that little creature is."

"I do, but I also found that the native women don't really need the Mongo."

"We know that. The problem is with the men." Azalee gently touched his penis and fondled it. Then she giggled. "I see you don't have such problems."

* * * *

Two days later, he went back to the *Lair of the Nine Serpents*.

Tessma greeted him with a happy smile. He knew she was fond of him and he hated himself for what he dad to do.

"I'd like to spend my time with you again," he said, taking her into his arms.

"I've been waiting for you," she whispered. Then she pulled him into one of the rooms.

Before he undressed, he said, "I have to use the lavatory first. Give me a minute."

"I'll be here." She smiled.

Inside the small room, he pulled out a thin rubber-like transparent tube, open at both ends. He pulled it over his penis.

It was a drug. The organic material would dissolve inside Tessma's vagina. Slowly, the warm inner flesh of her sexual organ would absorb it. Unconsciousness would follow soon after. She'd sleep for a couple of hours, long enough for him to get Brighteyes and then away.

He swallowed an antidote to counteract the effects of the drug on himself, and then he went back into the bedroom.

Tessma lay nude on the wide bed and smiled. "You're still dressed, you big tease," she pouted. Laughing, she jumped up and began to undress him. Then they tumbled onto the bed and he rolled between her inviting thighs. She kissed him passionately and moaned as his fingers caressed her body. Her hand traveled down to his belly, but before she could touch his erect penis, he entered her already dripping sheath.

She inhaled sharply. "Don't rush," she groaned between clenched teeth. Spreading her legs wider she allowed him to enter her deeper. "We have plenty of time. My brother is not here today."

Before he could answer, he felt the slight prodding of a mind touch.

I'm in position, lover. Azalee's thoughts were laced with amusement and something else.

You are jealous, he sent, also amused.

For a moment there was silence, then, *I guess I am. Just a little.*

Underneath him, Tessma was breathing hard, moaning, and clawing at his back.

It wouldn't be long now. He felt a stab of regret. She was very passionate. It could have been an enjoyable afternoon.

He climaxed and held her tight as she convulsed in the throes of her own orgasm. Then she lay suddenly still. He pulled out and felt her pulse. She'd be all right.

I'm ready, he transmitted.

You mean you're finished, came Azalee's answer. She had been in his mind all this time and he felt a slight tinge of embarrassment.

He dressed quickly and, after checking Tessma one more time, he left the room.

Brighteyes was not on her bed. Looking around, he couldn't find her.

"Damn it!" he swore, realizing he had made a mistake. He should have made certain the girl would be in her room. There was only one place she could be…in the bath. It was on the floor below.

Taking the stairs to the lower level, he walked cautiously down the corridor. He didn't know where exactly the bath was located, but he was confident he'd find it without any problems.

He knew her mind pattern and it shouldn't be too difficult to detect it. Carefully sending out searching thought tendrils, he made contact almost immediately.

There was no mistaking her familiar pattern. Her thoughts were confused, hazy, but she seemed happy.

Through her eyes, he saw the room she was in. She was half immersed in water, soap bubbles all around her. Another girl was scrubbing her back.

He saw other girls, some in the water, others lying under artificial sunlamps, drying their nude bodies.

There didn't seem to be any guards.

He withdrew from her mind, followed her mind impulses.

When he stood in front of the double doors leading into the bath, he stopped. Looking around, he found a closet with some robes. He found one that fit his large frame, and then he walked through the doors into the bath.

Some of the females watched him, as he walked in. A few, Brighteyes included, didn't pay him any attention.

He walked up to the woman who was scrubbing Brighteyes.

"Get her ready," he told her.

She gave him a suspicious look. "Who says so?"

"The big man himself." He smiled coldly. "Don't ask too many questions."

The girl led Brighteyes out of the water and began drying her with a large towel. Brighteyes giggled and rubbed herself against the other female.

"Hurry," Orion said. "He is not very patient."

She put a robe around Brighteyes. "Take her already."

"Thank you, Beautiful." He grinned with a leer, staring at her breasts. She was nude, like all the other girls. "Maybe I'll look you up the next time."

The girl didn't answer. Her face was expressionless, but she couldn't hide the fear in her eyes and her thoughts.

Even without touching her mind, he received the impulses of dread her brain transmitted.

Must be some kind of guy, this mysterious 'S'.

Orion's thoughts were grim as he took Brighteyes by the arm. She followed him eagerly, lost in her own fantasy world.

In the corridor, one of the men he had seen in the bar upstairs met him. He held a gun in his hand. "Where are you going with that girl?" he wanted to know.

Orion smiled, walking toward him. "I couldn't wait until she was finished with her bath." His mind contacted Azalee. *Trouble. I may have to come out in a hurry.*

"I found Tessma in her room. Unconscious. You got something to do with that?"

Orion shrugged, still walking.

The man at the end of the corridor aimed his weapon. "Stay back," he warned. "I have nervous fingers."

"Listen, friend." Orion sounded annoyed. "I paid good money for this girl. Is this the way paying customers are treated here?"

The man looked uncertain, lowered his gun.

Orion moved. He was still not close enough. Only the fact that he was faster and stronger than an ordinary man made it possible for him to reach his opponent before the man could bring up his gun again.

His shoulder smashed into the man's chest. Reaching for the wrist of the gun-hand, he twisted, felt bones and cartilage give away under his grip. The gun fell from the useless hand. They crashed to the floor, rolled, their limbs entangled. The man tried to gouge out Orion's eyes with crooked fingers.

There was no time for finesse, but Orion didn't want to kill. His thumb found the pressure point at the man's throat. Moments later, his opponent stopped struggling and went limp.

Orion stooped over him, checked his pulse, then he searched for the gun, found it and picked it up. Then he looked for Brighteyes.

She stood watching him without showing any interest. When she noticed his eyes on her, she smiled and came toward him, her arms reaching.

"Poor girl," Orion said, holding her for a short moment. Then he scooped her into his arms and ran toward the stairs, carrying her light body easily. Mounting the steps two at a time, his mind reached out for Azalee.

I'm coming out. Be ready.

He found the exit that led into the narrow back lane. Tessma had mentioned it after his casual inquiry. Hidden behind a curtained alcove, it was only meant as an emergency exit and not usually guarded. Unfortunately, not this time.

A little man stepped into his path, the muzzle of his big gun almost touching Orion's nose. "Not so fast," he said with a nasal voice. Seeing his face, Orion dubbed him immediately *Weaselface*.

He cursed himself for not scanning his surroundings. Hampered by Brighteyes, he froze.

"Did you really think you could walk out of here just like that?" the little man asked with a sneer.

"I guess I'm stupid." Orion sighed and stepped back slightly.

Weaselface followed, his gun unwavering. "Guess you are. This place is a fortress, friend. Everything is monitored; every exit, every room, even the girls. This one especially." The finger of his free hand touched Brighteyes's forehead. "The computer knows where she is and what she does every second of the day." He chuckled. "I should know. I'm the one who monitors her."

"I thought Tessma did that?" Orion asked.

The little man chuckled, again. "Usually, she does, but you can't trust a woman. I control the master screen. When she began switching off certain sections the computer registered this, of course, and it raised a red flag. So I began watching and I was not disappointed."

He grinned. "You two put on quite a show. I really enjoyed it."

"I'm glad you did," Orion said dryly. "It just proves again, you can't trust anyone, not even a computer. What's going to happen now?"

"To you? Stupid question. You've tried to rob my employer. He doesn't like that. You've been snooping around in one of his establishments. That he doesn't like, either. So what do you think is going to happen?"

"You employer, let's call him Mr. S, he doesn't like very much, does he?"

"You think you're pretty smart?" The eyes of the little man were icy. "After we've picked your brain, you won't feel so smug."

"What about Tessma?"

Weaselface shrugged. "Tessma? Not my decision. She made a big mistake. Got involved with a customer...on company time. She put us all in a vulnerable position. My employer..."

"I know, he doesn't like that," Orion finished for him. He took another step backwards. "Can I put her down? My arms are tiring."

"Put her down, but remember...I'm watching." His eyes were

unblinking behind the big gun.

Carefully, Orion began lowering the girl, then he dropped and, with Brighteyes still in his arms, he rolled to the side, past the little man.

He heard the soft *plop* as Azalee discharged her weapon, drilling a small hole into the little man's head. He had been so intend on watching Orion, he never noticed her coming through the exit door.

Without a sound, he fell forward, his weasel face covering part of his big gun.

"You've killed him," Orion said, unnecessarily.

"I did," Azalee said. "Had I given him the chance, he would have done the same to me. Now, let's get out of here."

Chapter Nineteen

"She's a beautiful woman. I can see why you care for her." Azalee gave Orion a little smile.

He returned her smile and took her hand. "You're just as beautiful, Azalee. Also, a bit more mature. She's very young."

Azalee shook her head. "Yes, I am beautiful, but there is a difference. She's human, I'm an alien. My beautiful body is artificial."

"Your body may have been artificially created, but it is still warm, living tissue, and your beauty lies elsewhere." He touched her mind, *saw* her real body, the creature who was Azalee. *As you've said, you're not human. Comparing yourself to a human would be unfair.*

She sighed, squeezing his hand. "Thank you, Hektor. The fact is I've lived in this body for so long, I've come to accept it as my own. That is our nature. Had our minds never touched, I would still find you attractive, and don't deny that this body of mine doesn't turn you on?" Watching his face, she opened her blouse to expose a pair of creamy breasts.

"You've made your point. I guess we are all conditioned to respond to external stimuli." He grinned. "You're a tease. You know damn well you are safe in this plush office."

Smiling, she closed her blouse. "I could always lock the door." She looked at Brighteyes who was stirring on the narrow couch. "It seems *Sleeping Beauty* awakes. I think it would be better if she didn't see you."

"Will she be alright?"

"I think so. She will be a little confused for a couple of days, but we'll keep her slightly sedated during that time. Whatever happened to her will be only a dream-like memory, soon forgotten." She gave him a sad smile. "I'm afraid you'll be part of that dream."

"That's all right. I don't want her to suffer from her experience." He touched the light spot on the girl's forehead where the transmitter had been attached. "A devilish device, but maybe a blessing in disguise."

"That and the drugs," Azalee agreed. "Otherwise, her mind may not have survived that trauma." She looked up and at the opening door, at the woman who appeared in it.

"He will see you now," the woman said. "I'll take care of the girl."

Orion and Azalee walked through the door into another office. It was lavishly furnished with heavy wooden furniture. Imported, of course. Wood like that didn't grow on Bakker's planet.

One wall was nothing but window, overlooking a vast ocean. On the beach, in the foreground, naked men and women were frolicking either in the water or on the white sand. High cliffs on one side broke the waves crashing against them and Orion could hear the faint roaring sound of the surf.

The man behind the huge wooden desk saw Orion studying the scene and chuckled. "An illusion, but it is the next best thing to being there."

He came around the desk, holding out a hand. "I am Thor Kirsten, and you are Hektor Orion. Pleased to meet you."

Orion shook the man's hand, felt the warm grip. Looking into his handsome face and into the dark eyes, Orion instinctively knew this man could be trusted. He sensed something else and was not overly surprised when the mind-touch came.

I know much about you, Thor Kirsten said, smiling.

You are like Azalee, Orion said, puzzled. *Your body is not a construct.*

"You are right, Azalee and I are members of the same species," Kirsten said aloud. "As to why I don't possess an android body is easy to explain. Normally, we don't take over the body of an intelligent being, not a live one."

"You look very much alive to me." Orion smiled with a touch of humor. "But how…?"

"When I was still a young man…maybe I should say when this body was young, the former owner died as the result of an accident. His brain was dead, but the body still alive. As it happened, some of my people were nearby. They recovered the body and removed the dead brain. Then they put me inside the empty cavity and Thor Kirsten was alive, again. This body is a fine, healthy specimen and I like it." His black eyes twinkled. "Nobody knew that the real Thor Kirsten had died. I became him."

"What about friends, relatives?"

"In a society depending on computers and artificial intelligence it is very easy to impersonate somebody else. I already looked like him,

143

so that part was easy, of course. I claimed temporary amnesia. While I *recovered*, my associates gathered all the information that was available of Kirsten and fed it into a computer."

"I understand." Orion nodded. "Information, like behavior, speech patterns, habits, life-experiences and so forth."

"Right. After having it all transferred into my own mind, I literally became Thor Kirsten."

"How many of your kind are on this planet?"

The older man looked at Orion. "I know what you're getting at, but don't worry, there are not enough of us to take over this planet. We're just happy to be able to blend in. We don't want to draw any attention to our presence here."

He walked over to a cabinet and opened it. Orion saw a number of bottles and glasses.

"Can I offer you something to drink? The best imports."

Orion accepted a glass and sank into one of the comfortable chairs. "Azalee didn't tell me much about you. I understand, she works for you. I guess I misunderstood when I assumed she was a government agent?"

"Oh, she is." Kirsten smiled. As president of CAMPOL, the second largest robot factory on Bakker's Planet, I am also head of Special Security, a sort of secret police force."

"Ah, the sweetness of power," Orion commented.

"Not so sweet. My hands are tied as far as ELCOM is concerned. We know that ELCOM manufactured those little robot-virgins. It is no secret. We also know now that one of ELCOM's sub-companies is responsible for installing the Mongos, but we can't prove anything."

He paused. "It might also interest you to know that your mysterious Mr. 'S' owns that company. His real name is Solm Thalson."

Azalee, who had been silent until now, smiled when she saw Orion's reaction. "You are correct to assume that he is the brother of Cal Thalson, ELCOM's Chief of Security."

"That explains why a couple of security men seemed so interested in my welfare," Orion said. "I'm beginning to see things a little clearer."

"That was the reason you couldn't stay at Dr. Kirku's laboratory. Cal Thalson practically runs the planet's regular police. He had all transmissions monitored, but even without that, he would have found you. Your only way to escape his detection was to disappear into the mountain."

Orion gave Azalee a crooked smile. "You know, I have to apologize to you. Somehow I suspected you to be involved."

She pouted, but her eyes were laughing. "After I let you pick my brains, you still didn't trust me. I'm disappointed."

"I have learned never to trust anyone completely, especially not a beautiful woman." Orion said, only half-jokingly.

Thor Kirsten laughed. "Can't say I blame you. Danger is usually hidden behind a beautiful façade."

Orion poured himself another drink. "I haven't really been briefed on the political situation on Bakker's Planet. I believe Azalee was supposed to fill me in, but things started happening so fast, she never got the chance to tell me much."

Azalee smiled wickedly, and then she winked. "You never gave me a chance to really talk."

Kirsten suppressed a smile. "Perhaps I can enlighten you. The big companies run Bakker's Planet. There are five of them. General Okten of ELCOM, our largest company, is also our illustrious leader. However, he is not a dictator, although he wouldn't mind to be one. The other four directors, I am one of them, would not allow that."

"Who controls the currency?"

"The banks, of course, but they are controlled by the government computer. They have no real power."

"Since you are the head of Special Security, you could easily be the real power here." Orion studied the other man thoughtfully.

Kirsten nodded. "I could be, but I'm not. My agents can investigate anyone, openly or secretly. They can even harass, but they can't make any arrests. Only the regular police can, upon our recommendation."

"There are other ways to get rid of somebody."

"Yes, there are, but my agents are not criminals."

Orion smiled. "I was only kidding."

"Maybe you were." Kirsten didn't smile. "You're coming from a different background, Mr. Orion. The nature of your occupation must have exposed you to many different societies, some lawful, others not. I know that you are a ruthless man. You have to be to survive, but I also know that you have respect for the law, if it is just."

"Who's to say what is just?" Orion didn't allow his eyes or face to show any expression. "More often than not the man behind the gun decides what is just."

"That is the reason you are here, Mr. Orion. Maybe you are *The Man behind the Gun*."

"I can't see how." Orion shrugged. "I haven't really done anything yet."

"Nothing that is obvious at first glance. But maybe just by being here you have set things in motion which would not have been exposed otherwise."

Thor Kirsten held out his hand. "It was a pleasure to meet you. Why don't you take it easy for a few days and relax. I don't think though that it is a good idea for you to stay in your hotel. Azalee will make arrangements for you to move into another hotel."

He walked Orion to the door. "And something else: Be careful. Thalson will not be pleased to find that native girl missing. He will be looking for you."

"I don't doubt that." Orion smiled grimly. "I'll watch out for him and his henchmen."

Chapter Twenty

They were waiting for him in his suite. Androids. Three of them.

He didn't know they were there until he entered his suite. Their artificial minds had not betrayed their presence. They wore the uniforms of the police force. Androids were expendable, but expensive to create, so they weren't taking any chances. They shot him with a nerve scrambler. He was unconscious before he hit the floor. When he regained consciousness, he was lying on a bed in a strange room.

"Welcome, Mr. Orion."

Orion turned his head to look at the speaker. He was young, good-looking.

"Please get up and follow me." The young man moved his hands with somewhat effeminate gestures. He opened the door. "They're waiting for you."

Orion groaned and held his head, trying unsuccessfully to quiet the terrible pounding inside his skull. That was the problem with the nerve scramblers. They were painless but had an unpleasant after effect.

Standing on shaky legs, he fought the slight dizziness, and then he grinned. "Lead on. Mustn't let them waiting. Whoever they are."

He was still alive. Not everything was lost. It did not greatly surprise him when he saw the large, beefy man behind the table.

Cal Thalson. Security Chief of ELCOM. Also, head of the planetary police force. The man beside him was equally large, equally beefy. It didn't take much to guess his identity.

Solm Thalson. The mysterious Mr. 'S'.

The other three people in the room were strangers. Two men and one woman. Startled, his eyes rested on the woman. She was not human. Humanoid, but definitely not human. Her eyes were large, blue with slit pupils. Her black hair was cropped close to her skull, leaving her pointy, tufted ears free. She looked familiar, at first. The resemblance was uncanny. Sheenah, the cat-woman he had known so intimately on Izzard-Junction, but it was not her. Sheenah's eyes had been green.

His gaze shifted back to Cal Thalson. "I hope you have a good explanation for abducting me."

The Security man didn't smile. His hard-looking eyes studied Orion coldly. "I don't need a reason, Mr. Orion, or whatever your name is."

Orion smiled. "It's been Orion ever since I was born. I never saw a reason to change it. I like the name."

"That may be so, but you are not Mendes Orion from the Planet Athena, unless you've undergone a rejuvenation process and added thirty centimeters to your height."

"Who says so?"

"I gave your credentials a better look. It struck me as odd that a merchant, even a rich merchant, from a small-unknown planet far away from here would have an account with a bank on Orando. The second thing that puzzled me was even stranger. I asked myself why a man like you would get involved with something as trivial as buying one hundred androids for sexual pleasure when you could buy any number of willing human or humanoid females."

"Maybe I'm a pervert," Orion suggested, grinning.

Thalson didn't seem to find any humor in that. "I think not, Mr. Orion. In addition, as a rich merchant you should be traveling with companions, guards, luxuries. You have neither. Really rich people will not take the chances you took. They usually live a pampered existence. They need luxurious surroundings."

"I'm a runaway from home, Mr. Thalson." Orion nodded." An eccentric. A bastard who likes to live dangerously. A disgrace to the family. At least that is what my father told me."

"Your father?"

"Yes. My father, Mendes Orion."

For the first time the shadow of a smile flickered over Cal Thalson's lips. "Very good, Mr. Orion, but not good enough. You are no more the son of this Mendes Orion than I am. He has never been married."

"I told you I was a bastard son."

Solm Thalson, who had been watching Orion, pounded his fist on the table. "Enough of this crazy talk! I don't really care who this guy is. He has taken something that belonged to me and he has killed one of my best men. I want him punished. He knows way too much already. So let's get rid of him!"

Cal Thalson shook his head. "Impatient, as usual, dear brother. We are not savages. Perhaps Mr. Orion can explain his actions and, who knows, we might even be able to work out a deal." He looked at

Orion with an almost friendly expression. "I hope you'll excuse my manners." He indicated the cat-woman. "This is Illra. She is a business associate and very interested in the Mongos."

"Yes, I am." She spoke Universal with the peculiar guttural accent typical for her species. "I am not familiar with this little creature. Have you had any experiences with the Mongo, Mr. Orion?" Her pointy teeth flashed white in her gray face.

Orion nodded. "Some."

While his attention was on the cat-woman, he suddenly felt the feathery touch of a mind probe. His shield snapped shut automatically, but then the touch was gone. He ruled out the woman, who he had suspected at first. As far as he could tell, it wasn't anybody present. The short touch had given him the impression of a strong mind. A dangerous mind.

"We'll talk again, Mr. Orion," Cal Thalson said. "Tomorrow."

They took him back to his room. He heard the click of an electronic lock and knew he was a prisoner.

On a small table beside the bed stood a tray with food and drink. Since he was hungry and there was nothing else to do, he consumed the food. Searching for sanitary facilities, he decided to try one of the other two doors. The first one led into a large but empty walk-in closet. Opening the second door, he suppressed a surprised sound. The room was larger than the one he occupied. Rich wood paneling covered the walls. In the center of the room, a huge tub was sunk into the floor. It was filled with water, the surface covered with thick soap bubbles. The soap-covered head and the slim shoulders of someone submerged in the water brought an automatic *Excuse me* to his lips. Then he walked boldly toward the tub, wondering who it might be.

At the sound of his voice, the person inside the tub turned toward him. "Hello, Orion," she said. "It seems we have adjoining rooms."

"Hello Illra." Orion grinned. "It does seem that way."

She ducked under the water to wash the soap from her head, and then she rose. He watched her lithe, glistening body emerge from the water. Slowly, she wiped the clinging foam from her high conical breasts. Her hands caressed the three smaller nipples below each breast, lingered on her belly, toyed with the thick black triangle covering her sex.

"The water is beautiful," she said, looking at him with large eyes. "Come in and join me."

He shrugged. "You know, that is a very good idea."

149

She watched him undress. When she saw his naked body, a sharp little tongue flickered between her white teeth. Then she laughed throatily and pulled him into the water. "Come on, let's have some fun. These business deals can become so boring."

Her hands rubbed over his strong chest, caressed his taut belly, and then, without preliminaries, she touched his penis. Her blue slit eyes were bright when she looked at him. "Is this thing just an appendix or can you use it for something other than eliminating liquid from your body?"

"Why don't you find out?" He grinned and boldly squeezed one of her breasts.

Playfully, she bit one of his shoulders, and then she kissed him on the mouth. Forcing her tongue between his teeth, she moaned when he grabbed her buttocks. Then she clamped her strong legs around him and, with one hand, she took his already stiff member and guided it between her legs. Without breaking the kiss, they managed to slip together. He sank his pole into her warm sheath with a sigh of relief.

The water sloshed over the rim of the tub as they thrashed around in the soapy liquid. After their first orgasm, Illra made him pull out. She rose and lay down on the wooden deck surrounding the tub, her legs still in the water. Pushing up her rump, she exposed the thick, swollen lips of her vagina beneath her plump buttocks and let Orion mount her from the rear.

The tub was just deep enough for him to stand and he slid easily into her soft love-channel.

"Ahh, that feels terrific," she moaned, as he pushed deep. His hands clasped her shoulders and, slowly, he moved behind her.

Her sexual appetite was as great as Sheenah's, the cat-woman he had known before. The fine fuzz that covered her slim body, glistened wetly, and he became aware of her faint, musky odor. It acted like an aphrodisiac and, remembering Sheenah, who had smelled the same way, his erection grew inside her. She cried out sharply as he increased his tempo. He flooded her again and she pushed her fleshy buttocks into his groin, her vagina pulsing over his shaft.

He pulled out, turned her around and onto her back and then he took her again on the wooden deck. She spread her legs wide and raked his back with sharp fingernails, as they hammered against each other. As the waves of pleasure rushed through his body for a third time and his defenses were down, the forceful entry of another entity into his mind came unexpected and like the blow of sledgehammer.

He screamed and fought for control, trying to push the intruder out of his mind. Having climaxed three times in a very short span had left his body weak, not taking into consideration that he had not yet sufficiently recovered from his encounter with the nerve scrambler. Unmoving, he lay in the woman's embrace, fighting for his life.

The intruder was strong, stronger than anybody Orion had ever confronted. Through his surprise attack, he had managed to enter deeply into Orion's mind and taken over part of his body. Orion rolled away from the woman, rolled toward the tub. He tried to stop it, but couldn't control his own body. He fell into the water.

Desperately, he fought to keep his mouth closed to keep the water from entering his lungs. When it seemed he was loosing the battle, something deep inside him awoke, something with terrible awesome powers. It rose up with a roar, easily pushed out the intruder, and tracked the fleeing thought tentacle.

The other mind closed up tight and erected an impenetrable barrier. Orion pulled back, closed his own mind. Then he rose out of the water. Illra stood looking at him. Her face showed no expression. Then, without warning, she threw herself at him. Both of them fell into the water. He knew what had happened. She was under control. The enemy was trying to get him through her.

Her arms and legs clamped around his torso, crushed him to her. Her sharp teeth searched for his throat. She displayed incredible strength and again he fought for his life. Her teeth sank into his shoulder, bit deep. The fingers of his right hand managed to dig into her pubic area; he squeezed hard, without results. Again, his head was under water, his lungs were ready to burst.

With one last desperate effort, his mind reached out for the woman, tried to break the other mind's control. Her limbs suddenly let go of him. He freed himself from her embrace and climbed out of the tub. Breathing hard and spitting water, he lay on the wooden floor.

He saw the cat-woman's shadow above him and rolled away, rose to his feet. Screaming, she sprang at him again, arms spread and fingers curled like claws. Her blue cat's eyes were wide open and crazy; her mouth was open, displaying her sharp teeth. He sidestepped her, grabbed her arm, and threw her across the floor. She crashed head first into the wall. Her body went limp.

He knew she was dead before he touched her. Hearing voices from the other room, he turned and looked at the two security men coming through the door, guns drawn. Then he looked at Cal Thalson.

"You killed her," Thalson said. "Is that how you repay my hospitality? First you rape a business associate of mine and then you murder her." He snapped his fingers. "Take him away and put him into more appropriate quarters!"

* * * *

After spending an unpleasant night in a cold, dark cell, he was brought in front of Cal Thalson again.

"We have to decide what to do with you, Mr. Orion."

"I think that decision has already been made," Orion said.

Two men entered through a side door, walked slowly into the room. One of them was elderly, short, haggard looking. The other one was even shorter, dwarf-like, his body bent and crooked. His head, with a huge cranium above a wrinkled, ugly face, was out of proportion to his grotesque body. Even though they had never met in person, Orion recognized him immediately the moment he looked into the man's large, oval shaped yellow eyes.

"I'd like you to meet Mr. Abram. He is from Apex," Cal Thalson said.

The elderly man bowed slightly. "So this is the man who is giving us all this trouble."

"Trouble, sir?" Orion asked. "I have the distinct feeling that most, if not all of this trouble has to do with you."

"How perceptive." Abram chuckled. "Pais tells me that you have a very unique mind."

Orion looked at the dwarf and said, "He should know. He's been snooping around in it."

"Aren't you curious to find out who Mr. Abram is?" Thalson asked.

"Since he is from Apex, I can guess. He is probably the one who ordered the special robot-virgins."

Abram laughed. "As I said, very perceptive. You are correct in assuming I'm responsible for that special order. Nice touch, wasn't it?"

"Why would you do something like that?"

"Well, well. I see no harm in telling you. There is very little chance of this information ever getting past these walls." He threw a glance at Thalson, who shrugged, but kept silent.

"I don't know if you are familiar with the geography of Apex, my home planet. Most of its surface is covered with high jagged mountains or dry, hot sandy wasteland. No rivers, no lakes, just deep crevices, and wide canyons. The only habitable area is at the poles, of which only the South Pole is of real importance and actually quite pleasant. It is owned and inhabited by a bunch of religious zealots. Five million of them."

"I gather you're not one of them," Orion stated dryly.

"Right again, my perceptive friend. I live on the North Pole; together with one million other unfortunates, by that I mean it is getting crowded."

"Why don't you move to the south?"

"We'd like to, but we don't practice the right religion."

"Then why not stay where you are and practice birth control," Orion suggested, chuckling.

Abram regarded him silently for a moment, and then he smiled. "You know, Orion, under different circumstances I might even get to like you. You seem to have a strange sense of humor." He coughed delicately. "It is not just the crowding. There are large Krill deposits in the south and those idiots don't want to dig them out of the ground. It's against their religion."

"Can't you respect that?"

"No, we can't. Most of our citizens live in poverty, barely able to scratch out a living, literally. If we can get rid of the government in the south and take over, we'd all be able to leave the poverty behind and live a life of luxury."

He shook his head in apparent dismay. "You know, most religions preach peace, not these people. Their priests are very militant. Fortunately, only the priests, the rest are sheep. If we can discredit the priests, ridicule them, their followers will soon stop believing in them. If they get mad enough, they'll lynch those priests, overthrow their government, and then we can step in as the good guys and lead them on to glorious riches."

"Who is *we*?"

"I and a couple of thousand disciples of the *True Church of Apex*. We'll make certain there'll be no more foul-ups like the one with the sex-driven virgins." He chuckled. "What a terrible and vicious thing to do."

"You're planning a stupid thing, Abram. If the hostages from Orando are killed, it will mean war between Apex and Orando. Apex will be wiped off the star maps."

"That can be averted. We will *discover* the people responsible and they will be punished. You can probably guess who the guilty ones will be, can't you?"

"The priests of course."

"Correct again. Who else? The people will be grateful to us. After we are in control, ELCOM will ship us a new supply of robot-virgins and in return, the company will be allowed to mine the Krill-crystals. Victory is already ours and I won't allow you to spoil it."

"I believe Mr. Orion gets the picture," Thalson said.

While Abram had been talking, the dwarf beside him had unsuccessfully tried to break through Orion's barrier.

"He is very strong," the dwarf said to Abram. "I don't know if I can get into his mind."

"There are other ways," Thalson assured him.

Orion sensed someone behind him, and then he felt the prick of a needle in his shoulder. The next thing he became aware of was the pressure of cool plastic against his bare back. He couldn't move. A tractor beam kept him immobile. A device above his head bombarded his mind with invisible rays.

"He is awake," a voice said beside him.

Orion couldn't see the speaker, but he recognized Pais's voice.

Again, he tried to enter Orion's mind. This time his attacks were much stronger. Orion knew the dwarf was using an artificial amplifier. The drug in his bloodstream had weakened him even more and the rays bombarding his brain seemed to thwart his ability to concentrate. His shield cracked. Pais was in. Silently, Orion fought against the intruder, tried to keep his sanity but felt himself slipping.

The dwarf made one fatal mistake. In his eagerness to destroy Orion, he gave too much of himself, entered too deep. When most of his identity was lodged in Orion's mind, Orion's alien self surfaced again and closed the trap. The dwarf screamed inside Orion's mind. Realizing the awesome power he faced, he tried frantically to fight his way out of the trap, but he failed. With one last desperate effort to escape, he died. The remnant of his identity was not strong enough to fight Orion. With ease, Orion took control over the dwarf's body.

"He is under my control," he said in the dwarf's voice. "Unfortunately, this man was very clever. He set a trap. When his personality died, it triggered the release of a deadly poison. He will die within two hours. I can't get any information from his memory. Unless we save him, he will be useless to us."

"The computer will find the antidote," Abram said.

"There is not enough time, we can't take the chance," Pais/Orion said, "but I know where the antidote is hidden. Somewhere in his hotel room."

"How do you know that?" Thalson watched the dwarf with suspicion in his eyes.

"The will to live is a survival trait of the human species. When the poison flowed into his veins, the location of the antidote popped into his awareness for a fleeting moment." Pais/Orion smiled. "I'd better get moving. I must take him with me. He is harmless now. I control his every action. However, I cannot safely animate his body while having to give all of my attention to my own. I can make him walk with help, but only one guard is needed to guide his body."

"Can we trust the dwarf?" Cal Thalson asked, looking at Abram.

The older man nodded. "I trust Pais with my life. Don't worry."

"Alright." Thalson spoke to one of the guards. "Get a skimmer ready."

Orion had spoken the truth when he told Thalson that he could only animate one body. He needed all of his concentration to control the body of the dwarf without arousing suspicion that something might be wrong.

As Pais, he walked to the skimmer and took the passenger seat. The guard followed more slowly, steadying Orion's real body and helped him into the backseat, and then he moved behind the controls in the front. Orion waited until they were far enough away from the ELCOM building.

"Stop the vehicle," he made Pais tell the guard.

"Why?" The guard threw him a suspicious glance.

"Just do so. I need to concentrate on the prisoner. My control seems to be slipping."

The guard shrugged and slowed down the skimmer. As soon as the vehicle stopped moving, Pais/Orion killed the guard with his own gun. The guard had been so intent on driving, he never noticed when Pais removed the gun from his holster.

Orion left the dwarf's mind and sat up. He was still naked. They hadn't even bothered to dress him. Getting the uniform off the dead guard proved difficult in the confines of the vehicle, but he managed.

Dressed, he left the skimmer with the two dead bodies and hailed a cab. Sinking into the soft seat, he smiled and relaxed.

Epilogue

Azalee stretched her voluptuous nude body. "The authorities on Apex have been notified and Mr. Abram will be received by a welcoming committee if he decides to return there. He is not an unknown on Apex. He and his disciples of the *True Church of Apex* have tried before."

"What about the hostages?" Orion asked.

"They have been released and the president of Orando thanks us for saving his daughter's life. Thor Kirsten thanks you for the successful completion of your mission. CAMPOL will be doing a lot of business with Orando from now on."

"What is going to happen with the Thalson brothers and ELCOM?"

"Now, that is a touchy subject. General Okten, our beloved leader, angrily denies any charges against his company. Ironically, the General himself is probably unaware of Cal Thalson's involvement. Thalson, of course, pleads innocence. In fact, he threatens to have Kirsten investigated by a third party. Listen to this…He charges Kirsten with conspiracy to take over Bakker's Planet."

Orion chuckled. "Strong charges."

"Kirsten can handle it and I believe Thalson will soon drop them anyway for lack of any real evidence. He knows damn well, if he makes waves, we will close down his brother's operation."

"Why don't you anyway? Those people are a bunch of dangerous criminals. Look what they did to me and that native girl, Brighteyes."

Azalee smiled. "He would just pop up somewhere else. Selm Thalson has many connections. He would be hard to convict." Her slim fingers toyed with the hair on his chest. "Strange, nobody other than my boss Mr. Kirsten mentioned you."

"I probably didn't leave any lasting impressions." Orion chuckled and, grinning, he put a hand over her breast.

She giggled and pulled him on top of her, spreading her legs. "Why not leave a lasting impression with me," she whispered into his ear. Then she kissed him tenderly. She sighed deeply as he entered her. As their bodies joined, their minds merged for one last time. *I love you, Orion.*

And I love you, Azalee.

The End